~~

ESCAPE

FROM

HANALEI

~~

ESCAPE
FROM
HANALEI

A NOVEL

EVERETT
PEACOCK

visit

everett.peacock.com

ISBN-13: 978-0615738345

ISBN-10: 0615738346

published by Hehunakai Books

hehunakai.com

Cover image:

Hanalei Moon, © Angela Treat Lyon 1985

http://Lyon-Art.com

proofing: Valentina Cano

v.1.1

~ other novels you might enjoy ~

~~

The Parrot Talks In Chocolate

The Life and Times of a Hawaiian Tiki Bar - book 1

~~

In the Middle of the Third Planet's Most

Wonderful of Oceans

The Life and Times of a Hawaiian Tiki Bar - book 2

~~

Tiwaka Goes to Waikiki

The Life and Times of a Hawaiian Tiki Bar - book 3

~~

Death by Facebook

~~

Escaping the Magnificent

~~

Skipping Rocks

~~

everett.peacock.com

~ ~ ~

pray for surf / happiness

~ ~ ~

Mahalos

How do you show significant appreciation for all the good things that have happened up to the point of this book's writing? Work backwards!

Big mahalos to the friendly people of Hanalei, those warm souls across the entire island of Kauai; the nice lady who rented us Hale Ha Ha O'Hanalei; tectonic plates shifting on cue, the volcanic haze, the numerous wild chickens and finally the spectacular tradewinds that eventually painted the entire scene in such vibrant colors and textures of warmth. And, of course, the full moon which I enjoyed immensely.

Hanahou! To the members of the now-annual "Geezer Fest" who attended, along with myself, this year's best one so far: Pat Kemp, David Lesperance, John Steinmiller and Tim Wheeler.

Thumbs up to those wonderfully patient people who helped me polish this novel so that my words won't bounce around in your head like a Kauai rooster at midnight: Glenn Stroup, Della Peacock and Valentina Cano.

To Angela Treat Lyon for having created an incredible image of beauty that she so graciously let me use on the cover, as well as doing the cover design.

A deep humbling bow to the twenty-foot surf, surging across Hanalei bay at midnight, for not sweeping us out to sea when we decided to bodysurf. To the fragrant kiawe-wood beach fire for sweetening the air, and for the unexpected hugs from the entire Sunday night crew at Tahiti Nui.

Double shaka to the members of the best house band I've ever had the pleasure to experience, "In Season" (always ripe), Chad Pa and friends.

Aloha for now! Mahalo forever!
Everett Peacock
Kula, Maui, Hawaii

one

~~~

Trish didn't realize her doorbell actually worked, but there it was again. The ancient brass bell clanged noisily, unfamiliar with anything pleasant or gracious. Frozen and ignored, it surely existed only to announce a rare obnoxious insistence.

Immediately she looked down at herself. Worn, matted UGG boots tried in vain to catch the cascading cloth of her pajama legs. A Chicago Cubs sweatshirt, probably new when they last won a pennant, swung from her shoulders. It would have to do.

No one had texted her about a visit. Nothing from Amazon was inbound. She sat her steaming coffee mug firmly on the wooden breakfast table. It was still heavy with caffeine. The clanging started again, finally breaking her curiosity into a thousand pieces of irritation.

"Hold on!"

The noise stopped so suddenly she now suspected someone's embarrassed hand might still be clutching the ice cold ring.

More brass, better lubricated, slid back on their bolts, latches and plungers, agreeing to release their captive master. Without a window on or near the door, she left two of the chains on and pulled open the heavy metal door.

A burst of icy air invaded the fragile bubble of warmth that had taken all morning to build up in her apartment.

"Mailman!" a half frozen face with a forced, apologetic smile announced.

Trish saw the uniform and the gray hair and felt secure enough to close the door, release the chains, and open the door wider.

"It wouldn't fit in your box," the old mailman said. "It's from Hawaii..."

Trish watched, amazed that the old man had trekked up the frozen steps from his heated mail truck, as he held a large painted coconut forward, gloved hands shaking vigorously with the cold.

"I'm going myself, ya know ..." he added, as Trish reached out into the cold to accept it. Another burst of cold pushed into her apartment and she quickly closed the door.

The coconut appeared frozen, like the rest of the world today, but the bright tropical colors painted over its entire surface still screamed out gaudy fun. Her name and address had been painted on the side and there was something that looked like a painted-on stamp as well.

Trish sat the gift down and went back to lock the door.

"Thank you!" she yelled through the door, the howling wind and the subzero temperatures. Her voice only bounced back. She had turned one lock and slid one chain before she decided to try again. Opening the door wide, standing in clothes that fluttered now like a parachute, she saw the old mail man just climbing back into his truck.

"Thank you, sir!" she yelled at the top of her voice.

Without turning, he used a considerable amount of energy to stop his hands from shaking long enough to slide closed the door. He was dressed for the weather quite properly, but it was something inside him that insisted he shake. A medical retirement in Hawaii was a great idea, and the painted coconut, having just arrived like a beacon of promise, prompted him to share some tiny part of his story. But she was impatient or the cold was too much. It didn't matter; it was her loss. She wouldn't get to hear how he had kept the coconut in his truck all morning, touching it often. She would never notice his frozen tears all over it, either.

The lady was waving so he tapped his horn twice, turned away and looked back down at his mail pile for the next stop. He wasn't going to scold himself, but it was probably far too late to really enjoy the tropics. At least, he thought, it would be a nice place to die.

His watch's face reflected an anxious glance again, without any complaint. One more hour until freedom. He looked back up to the lady's closed door, turned back to face the blowing snow and sped off - leaving a vapor trail of diesel fumes and disappointment.

two

~~~

The little poi dog stepped easily into the four inch deep concrete basin of water, wagged its butt a few times, and stepped promptly out. Most of the sand from the beach had rinsed off his feet.

Onolani did the same but got all the sand off of hers.

She decided to skip the outdoor shower until the papaya picking was done. Her big straw shade hat would hold all she could eat for breakfast as well as the solitary lime that would liven up the pink succulent flesh.

The little mixed-breed, or "poi", dog followed her, staying just outside her shadow in the comfortable warmth of a building morning brightness. Except for a few distracting geckos scurrying about ahead of the both of them, the little dog watched her closely. A quirk of nature had given him full color vision, and Onolani's brightly painted pareo mesmerized him.

He watched her walk around to the back of her modest two-story wooden home, stepping through the long shadows of her papaya tree patch. Shaking his head a few times did nothing to clear his mind of the vibrant colors not just hanging off of his master's hips, but all around him. Greens shouted out in every possible shade, blues in the sky framed themselves in brilliant white clouds and below them all, every primary color combination was breathing life into all manner of flowers.

His own browns and blacks seemed to shimmer in the light as he leapt from one patch of sunlight to another, following Onolani.

Even the chickens that patrolled between the papaya trees for bugs were rainbow colored. Several baby chicks took notice of him, as if they might play with him. He knew better. Although the chicks were great fun to chase, the hens were far better at chasing *him*. The roosters, worse yet in their loud reds, greens and yellows, simply hypnotized him into a quivering mass of fur that they then easily pecked and punished.

"Come on, Poi," his master said, walking farther to pick another ripe papaya. He ignored her speech impediment, knowing she was trying to call him "boy." It was fine, he could overlook such things. She fed him, took him for long walks along the beach and let him sleep in the house. Life was good. Amen.

Running around to the open yard facing the majestic jungle peaks above Hanalei he found Onolani waiting for him in her chair. An open papaya was accepting the juice of another willing lime, which meant his treat was certainly next. He sat patiently at her feet, ignoring the chickens close by.

Sure enough, she reached down and gave him a piece of pork, rubbed behind his ears and said, "Good boy!"

Poi wagged his butt in celebration, knowing she would always keep trying until she said his name right; and for that he loved her beyond his capacity to ever understand.

three

~~~

Way up Wai'ale'ale way, on the top of Kauai, some 5,000 feet
above the surf, the small lake by the same name was catching rain.
Lots of rain. So much so that it lived up to its name and was
overflowing. Gushing really, over small ledges at first, then moving
deeper and deeper into the valleys that reached into the heart of the
island. Carefully, methodically, it continued carving dimensions into the
long dormant rock. The water moved swiftly over higher and higher
ledges, cascading dozens and then hundreds of feet, catching the
same morning light Onolani and Poi were appreciating. Rainbows, most
of them unseen, twinkled like children among the merry drops now
flying independently in the wind's updrafts and swirls.

Much of this rainwater from the night before had finally made it
down the long, winding Hanalei River and into the taro patch just across
the street from town. There, the old hippie everyone knew as Birdman
stood barefoot facing Wai'ale'ale, long gray hair unfettered, shirtless, an
electric guitar in hand. Strapped to his waist, just above his well-worn
Dick Brewer surf shorts was a small portable amp. Noise canceling
headphones completely covered his ears, the wire snaking around
behind him to the amp.

Everyone off to work this early in the morning was quite used to
seeing him every morning it wasn't pouring rain. Every morning they
glanced over to see his familiar grin facing the mountains. Some said
he used to be a preacher man who had lost his congregation; others

said he had taken too many wipeouts surfing at Tunnels. Most found comfort in his consistency. Ching Young Grocery found his reliable appearance each day stacking bananas, breadfruit, boxes and cans to be worthy of forty hours a week.

~~~

Onolani and Poi, fresh from their papaya and pork breakfast, sat at Auntie Lolo's Coffee & Cream and watched him. His reverence was silent, yet he moved his hips to some unheard rhythm only he and God could hear, and maybe by some twist of quantum mechanics, the mountains themselves as well. His old, yet still strong, tanned shoulders rocked the guitar as he channeled Jimi Hendrix, Eric Clapton and whatever tropical blues he was working on by himself.

Onolani watched him intently, silently tapping her foot to his rhythm, loving how he was grooving to his own *personal spiritual manifestation*. Of course, those three words were overused lately in the yoga studios and franchised meditation parlors, but she didn't let the uninitiated marketers ruin them for her. Those three words defined her as well, had opened up the very heavens to her. Having spent the majority of her life living there, she knew an angel when she saw one. Birdman wasn't one, but there was one real close to him.

Inspired, she opened her bamboo cloth backpack, pulled out an organic ink pen, some hemp stationary and began to write to her sister.

"*Dearest Trish,*

I hope you found the coconut fun! It actually fell into my yard a few weeks ago. Kainalu and I were just sitting there talking about you and boom! It fell. We knew it was a sign from the great Cosmic Gift Giver, something we had to share with you.

I really hope you will visit soon, winter here is wonderful. The days are filled with so many wonders. Papaya gets sweeter, the ocean sings all day and night, the birds learn new songs, interesting people come into town.

It must be cold there, at your place, now.

You know... now that Mom is gone... and Dad - there is no one left to berate you (like they did to me) for coming to paradise and doing absolutely nothing. So... come soak up the magic with me...

I miss you terribly, please come to Hanalei... it's only us now.

Love,

Onolani

(I've taken this name now that Mom is gone, Teresa never felt right, you know?)"

Onolani reached down to pet Poi as she re-read her letter.

"Good boy," she whispered just as she noticed Birdman, across the street in the taro field, sit his guitar down on high ground, reach up with his muscular arms to braid his hair, then slide his Hanalei Surf shirt over it all. He was still handsome. It had been a couple of decades since they had last been lovers, but on that point, time had not etched away any of the memories. He turned away from the mountains, picked up his gear and walked across the street toward the grocery store.

"Big boy," she whispered a little louder, watching Birdman and still petting Poi. The little dog was ecstatic, wagging his butt so furiously he fell off the picnic table bench.

four

~~~

Invitations to come to Kauai were going out to others as well. Despite the smog, traffic, brush fires, and jobs that could suck the life out of you, the U.S. Mail still made Special Deliveries to Santa Ana, California.

Geologist David Lesperance didn't know he even had a door-bell, but there it was, buzzing halfheartedly. Home for a long lunch, he was debating finishing up his reports without going back to the office, yet the office had somehow found him. The door bell rang again.

He peeked out the window, saw the U.S. Postal colors on a hybrid truck, a uniform standing at his door, and took a deep breath. In his business, such visits often required a signature, and signatures often required a great deal of thought, analysis and lawsuit avoidance.

Most of his work required disaster analysis: is that fuel tank going to leak in the next three years; is this old gas station going to spill petroleum products into the ground water; are these overpriced cliff homes going to slip into the Pacific? The vast majority of those answers were "yes", but saying so without God's thumbprint usually garnered a lawsuit. If someone was going to lose millions of dollars because of his opinion, then his opinion usually became Exhibit #1.

"Special delivery, Mister Lesperance."

Dave looked around the curtain again. The mail lady was better described as a mail girl. She might be nineteen but that was being generous. Dark, Hispanic features hid her true age well. Her smile showed she felt comfortable with whatever direction people guessed. Dave took the electronic signature pad and gave it his usual flourish of nonsensical letters.

"So, how's it hanging, Mister Lesperance?"

Dave looked up at her after handing back the device, his eyebrows near his hairline in surprise. "Pardon me?"

She smiled broadly. "You know, over the cliff?"

Dave shook his head, still confused.

"I saw you on public TV, testifying about those cliff houses sliding into the ocean." She shifted her stance to her other foot and stood a little taller. "You said they were hanging on with slippery hands," she paused and then looked him directly in the eyes. "You looked great."

"Thank you..." he glanced at her name tag quickly. "Henrietta."

"You know, if you ever need any help, I'm your girl," Henrietta said, thrusting her chest out unconsciously. "I can carry your bag; clean up after, whatever you need."

Dave took a step back off the porch, one foot back inside his protective shell. "Thank you for the offer, Henrietta. Uh - I will keep that in mind..."

"Here's my number," she thrust an undelivered flier for a new fitness club into his hands, magic marker written broadly next to a vivacious woman in the ad. "If my grandmama answers, just tell her you'll call back later. Don't leave your name; she's very protective, you know."

"OK," Dave said, moving backwards faster now. "Bye now," he said, looking across the street for a hidden film crew or an FBI van. His door closed without her moving an inch. He peered out the window, waiting for her to leave, but she only reached into her pocket , pulled something out and left it on his door knob.

There had to be a rule about dating government employees he figured. He had several government contracts, mostly on decommissioned military bases in the area, and somewhere, somehow, there was no doubt a clause about such improprieties.

Finally, she walked back to her mail truck, swinging her hips for what she bet were his spying eyes. Dave did her the honor of taking that bet, smiling when she finally drove away. Immediately, he walked to his door, opened it and found on the door knob a picture of her in a bikini.

"Geez," he whispered to himself. He stuck the picture in his right pocket.

Eventually, he remembered the envelope she had delivered. It had a State of Hawaii seal in the top left corner. The envelope opened easily.

"Dear Mr. Lesperance," it began. He scanned it quickly. It was a job offer, one that he had apparently applied for, but it'd been so long ago he had forgotten.

"Your application for surveying and recommending new tsunami inundation maps for the island of Kauai has been accepted. We require you finish by December 15, so that the new maps can be included in the following year's phone books.

Please confirm your bid, completion date and include your required insurance documentation."

It was signed "Hawaii Civil Defense" and had a raised embossed seal there as well. He sat down on his couch and thought back a year or so.

Now he remembered this gig. He had already completed most of what he needed just by preparing the bid. Detailed satellite elevation maps for the entire State of Hawaii coupled with the new USGS earthquake average for the Pacific rim plugged into his laptop had drawn him new "high water" marks in about two minutes. It was rough, but for the most part presentable. All he had to do was visually survey the coast at selected points to confirm the satellite data was accurate. Easy money and a trip to Hawaii!

Now all he had to do is figure out which of the islands there was called Kauai.

five

~~~

The one forgotten problem with paradise, or in this case Hanalei, is that it behaves a lot like a magnet or a cosmic black hole. It'll suck you in easily, but it's quite difficult to leave. Most people manage to get away with only a few tears, or a few complaints about going "back to reality", or even excuses about how something in the world back home needed them. Despite their resolve, determination or justifications, there is a discernible pain in leaving that, frays the edges of their souls.

The road from paradise to "back home" most certainly runs along the very outskirts of hell. And the first stop is the Lihue airport, the saddest place on the Earth.

The boarding areas are still with disappointment. People sit uneasily in the plastic chairs, thinking that the one vacation that had finally given them a sense of something really special was at its end. Gloominess permeates their long faces. All of them are quietly thinking that if life had dealt them a slightly better hand, they wouldn't have to go back to... wouldn't need to... wouldn't ever have to wonder about the rest of the world.

It was most difficult on the teenagers. The adults could deal with the spiritual hangover and the little kids were simply looking forward to another plane ride. But those who still had a choice in the direction their lives might take could feel a tinge of panic. They had tasted the salty surf, swam naked in the waterfalls, and sucked the sweet juice from a freshly picked lilikoi on a warm morning hike to the mountains.

24

They had seen the happy excitement in the eyes of the local kids who lived there, the ones that greeted them with knowing smiles - silent manifestations of the magic that washed their souls every day.

People arriving, like Pat Kemp, had little indication that such magic was close at hand. Multiple time zones and slower than necessary airplanes had worn him down. The trip had been anything but wonderful. His ukulele case had been strip-searched in Dallas, and the approach to landing on Kauai had been less than spectacular. His new home looked a little dry, like Texas, and honestly a bit flat, save for a few distant mountains. The air was a bit humid, and almost... hot. Wild chickens littered the rental car lots while baby chicks spilled over onto the one lane airport exit road.

Mainland airports rarely had much in the way of happy, vacation weary tourists but he expected to at least see some here. However, all he saw were bummed out people staring out the big plate glass windows at the departure gates, or kids crying on the rental car bus. It was a bad sign immediately impressed upon all who were arriving - maybe this place sucked?

The workers at baggage claim and Hertz were friendly enough though, even laughing and joking with him, offering him a free chicken with his convertible upgrade.

"Really? A free chicken?" Pat asked looking around at the dozens of colorful birds pecking after pebbles on the asphalt lot.

"Yeah, brah, we get plenty!" The young man proclaimed, his half-smile indicating this was a prank. "Pick any one you like!"

Pat declined. Somehow, he suspected there would be plenty of chickens everywhere he went on this island. Maybe he could add some specialty chicken dishes to the menu of Tahiti Nui - the Hanalei bar he had just purchased, sight unseen.

~~~

Poi loved car rides. It was the only time he could go that fast and not get tired. Short little legs provided a closeness to the 'aina that he did truly appreciate, but the tradeoff was speed. Plus, Onolani, God bless her, always played music he could wiggle his butt to as he stood up on the seat and out into the wind of the open passenger window.

He closed his eyes against the rainbow of colors. After a deep breath, he sniffed the myriad selection of smells rushing past him that began with ripe fruit in Hanalei, transitioned to sweet grasses near Anahola, and then to salt mists as they drove past the beaches of Kapa'a. A full hour after leaving home, he was sneezing at the car exhaust in traffic near Lihue. Finally, when Onolani stopped for the cheap Costco gas he simply had to get on the floor to hide from the fumes of that primitive fuel those poor humans still embraced.

"Almost there, Poi," Onolani announced, prompting Poi to jump back up on the seat and resume his tasting of a different wind. The colors, too, were quite a bit different than back in Hanalei. Here the greens were lighter, and the blue sky a bit paler. The buildings all seemed to have a light dusting of red dirt. In fact, some enterprising humans were actually charging money for Red Dirt t-shirts. That was cool by Poi, like making lemonade if you had only lemons, or making a Coco Loco Moco if all you had were coconuts... and rum. Onolani had a lot of coconuts. Her friends had a lot of rum.

"There she is!" Onolani yelled, braking hard and sending Poi to the floor again. She stopped right out in middle of the no-stopping lane in front of the open-air baggage claim area. Jumping out and leaving her door wide open, blocking the entire lane now, she ran around the front of the truck and flew into the arms of what Poi thought was one of the most battle-weary people he had ever seen.

"Trish," Onolani sang into her younger sister's shoulder length hair. "How are you?"

She knew the answer was surely somewhere south of "not good" and only a little north of "near death". Trish was pale, hunched over in exhaustion and obviously in the throes of a massive rhinovirus attack.

"Oh, Teres…" she almost said before a body-shaking sneeze left her speechless.

People close by diverted to the sides of the sisters, and the security guard, instead of chasing Onolani out of the no-stopping zone, indicated to her that perhaps quarantine was best for her sick traveler. He wrapped his neck bandana around his mouth and nose and raised an eyebrow until Onolani nodded.

"Let me take your bags, honey." She heaved the single over-weight behemoth into the truck bed, opened the passenger door and helped Trish in, even buckling her seatbelt for her. Running around to the driver's side and waving to the security guard she found Poi nervously licking Trish's hand.

"I'm sorry I'm in such bad shape, Teresa." Trish paused. "I mean…"

"Onolani." Onolani smiled. This moment had been coming for a very long time. "Ono... it means good. And, lani," she turned to look her sister directly in her watery eyes "... means beautiful."

Trish smiled weakly. "Onolani. I like it." Quickly, she brought a tissue up to her nose, and sneezed.

Poi took a step back, looked over at his master for some kind of nonverbal signal, found only pity, and so went back to licking Trish's free hand.

"My flights were horrible," Trish whined. "Delayed out of Chicago, back to the gate twice and bumpy all the way to the gate here." Trish wanted to continue complaining but was distracted by something outside as they drove through Lihue.

"Those... are they chickens? They're so colorful!" She sneezed before she could continue.

"Sure are," Onolani answered.

Trish sniffled and asked, "Did they escape from the zoo?"

Onolani laughed warmly, happy to have her mainland sister here. "No, honey. They didn't escape."

~~~

Pat sat for a moment in the skinny emergency lane and looked around. It had to be the most beautiful spot he had ever broken down on. As he got out of the convertible, he corrected himself. This was not a breakdown, it was a crash. Red convertible against several large chickens. He looked under the car, opened the hood and saw the problem. Fan belts and spark plug wires didn't play well with body parts. The battle had been gruesome.

Fresh into retirement from making his millions in the defense industry, he had learned one fact of war: both teams lost. In this case it was both the chickens and the red convertible. The eventual winner, if there was one, was always the team that could be repaired.

His cell phone had no signal, of course. It might have been Murphy's Law, but it was most likely the fact that he was in the middle and at the bottom of a long bridge crossing a deep valley. He thought about walking out to get a signal so he could call a tow truck or the rental guys. Murphy's Law though, did finally manifest in the fact that when one is at the bottom of such a bridge, it's uphill in both directions.

Pat reached into the car to punch on his emergency blinkers, popped open his trunk and walked back to survey his luggage. One had lost a wheel in transit somehow and the other, although a shoulder bag, was far too heavy to hump up a hill.

He sat on the back bumper of his car and threw up his hands. "I should've taken that free chicken!"

~~~

Onolani and Poi were snuggled together as Trish slept against her window. The drive back home was quiet. The truck was behaving well, humming right along, enjoying the inexpensive gas and the fact that it too was headed back to the north shore.

As they started down the long Kahiliwai Bridge Onolani saw the emergency blinkers and a tall man throwing his hands up into the air.

"Hitchhiker, Poi," Onolani whispered. "We gotta pull over and give him a ride."

Poi immediately stood up on her lap and peered over the dashboard to assess the hitchhiker. He knew his one true mission in life, besides taking long walks on the beach, was to protect his master and to this task he was seriously committed.

The guy was easily a tourist: in clean clothes, a car with very little red dirt on it and suitcases in the back of an open trunk. However, Poi noticed he did not have his thumb out looking for a ride. It was time to whimper a little and let his master know he had some reservations about that suspicious fact.

"It's OK, Poi," she whispered, already stopped and opening her door to get out. "He needs a ride, anyhow."

Pat was surveying Onolani as well. Last time he had broken down the guys that pulled up had robbed him. It had cost him hundreds in cash, all of his luggage and a broken tooth. However, this lady wasn't carrying a crowbar.

"The view is pretty nice from here, isn't it?" Onolani offered walking up to Pat, hands on her hips. "But, you need a ride, don't you?"

Pat let out a deep sigh; it looked like Kauai was going to be comfortably friendly. "Well, I have to admit," he said with a big grin. "The view just got a lot better!"

Onolani blushed. "Yeah, you're right. But, you still gotta ride in the back of the truck. Throw your bags in there. We're going all the way..." she paused and shot him a mischievous smile. "... to Hanalei."

In a minute, his bags stored next to Trish's, Pat was seated backwards in the bed of the truck, up against the window.

Trish stirred and woke as they climbed out of the next valley. She startled a little when she saw Pat in the back of the truck.

"Ono, who's that guy next to my luggage?"

Onolani smiled patiently. She expected some level of anxiousness from her mainland sister. Kauai would take several days to mellow her out.

"He's a hitchhiker; his car broke down back there."

"Seriously, a stranger? You picked up a stranger?" Trish kept turning back and forth, looking at the back of Pat's head and then to her sister and her big infectious smile.

"All hitchhikers are strangers, Trish. Otherwise they're just a friend you're giving a ride to." Onolani nodded silently to herself as the logic of that statement sank in.

Trish, exasperated from her cold, her long journey and what she now knew was going to be some adjustment to her hippie sister's way of life, sat back heavily in her seat.

"Where's Poi, then?" Trish asked, her eyes closed against the answer.

Onolani laughed. "Oh, he's back there guarding the luggage and keeping an eye on that stranger."

In her rear-view mirror Onolani watched as Poi stood against the side of the truck bed, head out into the slipstream, sniffing.

Poi, always willing to relocate into the back of a truck, was happy to be where he could better smell the wind. Very soon thereafter he caught a hint of the fragrant fruit smells in Hanalei.

six

~~~

Onolani was trailing behind six rental Jeeps, all blue, crossing the one-lane Hanalei Bridge together like an invading army. Two old Ford pickups patiently waited on the other side, hunting dogs poking their snouts out from their cages.

Poi crossed to the opposite side of the truck bed as they passed the Fords, trying to be perfectly still. He averted his eyes. Hunting dogs would never bite him, this he knew, but they were the wildest of his kind, *wild like Vegas*. If he ran with them even once, he would most certainly end up a changed animal - at something close to the molecular level. All would be lost as domestication slipped away forever. He had had many dreams of wild pig hunts through mud and jungle. He frequently daydreamed of running with the big dogs! Yet, big dogs, like Vegas, could take more than they gave. Poi understood very well, as he continued to ignore the hunting dogs, that the best strategy to avoid temptation was to pretend it didn't exist.

It was but another minute before the t-shirt shops and kayak rental joints appeared. A lone real estate office had its windows wallpapered with tourist-priced single-wall constructed kit homes. Couples from faraway places walked hand in hand along the narrow dirt strips bordering the asphalt, ever faithful that no car would stray two feet to the side and strike them.

Pat was standing up in the pickup bed now, leaning on the top of the truck cab, flashing back to American Graffiti - remote tropical island style - with chickens. Except perhaps that it was an even smaller town.

"Hey, there she is!" He shouted, standing up straight and pointing at the simple, un-lit "Tahiti Nui" sign, tucked directly under the overhanging "Tiki Man Pizza" board.

Draped just under both of them was a hand-painted bed sheet. Black paint scrawled "Hui Meeting T-nite", while red paint had succeeded at getting a hibiscus rendition tucked into the corner. Pat noticed an already full outside deck of people holding beer bottles and it wasn't even dark outside yet.

At the next corner, was a tiny Hertz Rent-a-Car sign.

Pat tapped hard on the roof twice.

"Hey, stop here a second," he yelled.

The truck pulled over just as a group of big-tire beach cruiser bicycles rolled single file in their lane going the opposite way.

Pat stuck his head in Trish's window, smiled broadly at her for just a split second before glancing over to Onolani.

"Be back in thirty seconds! Promise."

He turned and ran up the two wooden stairs where he found the clerk looking up from his magazine.

Throwing the keys up onto the counter, he pointed out of town. "Big ass bridge, four or five miles, that way."

Turning to run back out, he stopped and added, "You won; it can be repaired."

~~~

Hale Ha Ha O'Hanalei, as it said on the wooden plaque hanging outside Onolani's simple home, got Trish to giggling. The garden art, melted bottles of various colors, succulents, flowering cacti, moss hanging off plumeria trees and stately papaya trees told her it was no joke - she was not in Chicago anymore, and here Toto was called Poi.

"You might want to rest a while, but I'm going to walk over to the Hui meeting; tonight's really important," Onolani said, hurrying around her kitchen like she had forgotten all about it and now just remembered.

"Sure," Trish said, dropping her purse on the expansive punee bed out in the TV room. "All I need is a remote control and a stiff drink."

"Remote's on the bamboo tray there." Onolani pointed as she wrapped a fresh pareo around her. "And the cabinet has rum. Juice in the refrigerator." She stopped as she stepped into her slippers. "You sure you're OK? I hate to run, but tonight is about the new tsunami inundation maps."

Trish was already three ice-cubes into making her first drink. "Sue what?"

"Tidal wave," Onolani simplified. "Some California geologist is coming to town with the intent to redraw the high water marks. Everyone's upset."

Pouring by sight only, Trish filled the high ball glass to the rim, leaned over to sip the excess out and turned to her sister. "What's up with that?" She had searched specifically for those words to replace the "So what?" that first popped into her mind.

"Higher lines up the beach means more houses and businesses get included in the designated "disaster-zone". Insurance goes sky high, permitting anything new becomes impossible. Most folks think it's just a ploy to price out the few remaining beach-house owners who haven't sold out to…"

Trish caught the pause and waited. She was stuck trying to guess the word. The implication though was out-of-towners.

"Doesn't matter what the rumors are," Onolani said. "It's always a good time to talk story, or gossip or politics at Tahiti Nui. At the end of the night everyone hugs everyone else anyhow."

Trish flashed on a long forgotten fact about her and Onolani's mom as she took her second long drink. Was Onolani a drinker too, hanging out nightly in bars, like her mom used to? Or was she a stay at home lush like she was becoming in Chicago?

"Just show me the security system, and I'll take a good nap here in front of CNN or whatever movie channel you have." Trish kicked off her shoes as the rum began having the desired medicinal effect on her cold.

Onolani paused again. She put her flashlight down, grabbed a glass and poured an inch of rum. She tipped it up and held it until it was drained. The cup sounded hollow as it found the counter. It didn't ask for more.

Catching Trish's eye she started her sister's indoctrination into rural Hawaiian life. She had hoped it wouldn't be too shocking, too soon.

"Sister, there's no lock on the door. There's no cable or satellite TV, either. I do have a nice selection of DVDs under the TV, and there must be a hundred books on the shelves."

Trish was looking around as if someone might be breaking in at that very moment.

"No lock on the door?" She whispered, afraid to alert any would-be prowlers to come on in.

"Your security system, though, is quite robust," Onolani said proudly, her hands resting comfortably on her hips.

"Thank God!" Trish said. "How do I work it, then?"

Onolani reached into the cabinet above the sink, pulled down a zip lock bag full of brown strips and threw it over to Trish.

"Feed Poi one of these every hour and he'll take a bullet for you."

~~~

The twenty-two year old brunette from Phoenix was laughing at practically every joke her stand-up paddling instructor/realtor told her. She was getting the feeling that they would end up in his Jacuzzi after all.

"Honey, they don't call me John Steinmiller for nothing!" John sat back in his chair, waiting. If she laughed at that one she really was drunk. If not, then he might chance swimming with her in the bay tonight. Having learned his lesson the hard way, he never wanted to resuscitate a girl who was throwing up Mai Tais and seawater again.

The brunette leaned over the table toward John, splashing her Mai Tai onto the napkin. "You crack me up!" She was a little loud but it got her point across.

"I appreciate that, darling," John said, standing up. He turned and walked up to the small stage reserved for the band, or anyone else brave enough to be the center of attention.

He tapped the microphone twice getting the two amplified echoes he was looking for. "Ladies and gentlemen, let's get this meeting going, shall we?" He looked over to his date and winked. She looked to be drooling a little, so John focused again on the crowd of twenty or thirty people.

"Folks, I'm your local Aloha Da Kine Realtor, John Steinmiller." He waited a few seconds for any applause. Only his date was standing up and clapping furiously, and everyone else was silently watching her. The bartender nodded and raised an empty glass in his direction.

John nodded back. "Tonight, we need to talk about that California guy coming over here to disrupt things." That got a big round of boos and several bottles banging against their tables.

"Yeah, that's right. Disruption we don't need. Our current tsunami inundation maps are just fine." He gracefully took the full beer mug from the bartender who had walked it over. "Some boneheads in Honolulu got it into their noggins that the entire state needs updated maps."

"We don't need no stinking maps!" Someone back on the deck yelled out. Then they corrected themselves, "...updated maps!"

"No way!" Another voice on the deck added.

"That's right folks, but here it comes anyhow," John said. "What we gotta do is make sure this guy doesn't make one mistake, doesn't go off and *estimate* anything! We want atomic time clock accuracy!"

The brunette began laughing at "atomic time clock", thinking John was telling another joke. The rest of the bar waited for him to explain a little further.

"We gotta keep an eye on this guy as he goes about his business, ask him questions, engage him as best we can. Basically," he stopped, tipped the beer up for a quick two chugs, wiped his lips and continued. "We gotta keep this guy honest!"

Everyone clapped at that. John bowed and signaled the bartender for another.

"When is he coming?" Someone shouted from the bar.

"Tomorrow," John said, checking his notes.

"What's he look like?" The same voice asked.

"I don't know, but my guess is he'll blend in right up to the point where he pulls out whatever it is a geologist pulls out."

"A hard hat?" the brunette shouted.

Laughter erupted and John winked at his date. "That would be a sure sign indeed!"

"How long is he gonna be around?" Another voice asked, this time from the direction of the kitchen. It was the cook.

"Last I heard, he's got himself an office in Ching Young Village somewhere, probably the doughnut shop that just cleared out, next to Hanalei Surf."

Murmurs and whispers bounced around the bar as everyone soaked that up. It sounded longer than anyone had expected.

"Couple or three weeks," John added. He's based here in Hanalei as he surveys the entire island. He'll be flying around on Air Kauai at least once a day."

"Helicopter tour every day!" The cook said, disgusted. He turned and walked back into the kitchen.

"Sounds like a vacation to me!" Another voice from the deck threw out.

John finished his first mug of beer and traded it with the bartender as he finished up.

"Look, we got no beef with this guy, whoever he is. Let's keep that straight. We only got a beef with higher tsunami lines, which by the way, will most certainly include this beloved bar. If science insists we all live in fifteen foot pole houses, then as far as I'm concerned they can pay for it. Personally, I like tree-houses!"

That got a round of laughs from the crowd and John took it as a sign, sitting back down with his date.

"How'd I do, baby?" John asked reaching for her hand.

She just shook her head, amazed that her vacation had taken such a romantic turn, right before she had to fly home.

"Is your Jacuzzi warm?" She almost whispered it out of fear of sounding too desperate.

Before John could answer that yes it was and that it even had life vests as well, a man walked silently up to their table. He sat down without an invitation.

"Mister Steinmiller," he said abruptly.

John took the intrusion lightly, as any good salesman would.

"What's up?"

"Cecil," the man said, as if he only needed one name.

John sized him up immediately. He was no Elvis, Madonna or Gaga.

Cecil ignored the fact that John didn't recognize him and launched into his complaint.

"Rumor has it the USGS is going very conservative with their estimates after those last two big tsunami in Indonesia and Japan."

"That they may, sir." John was trying to think where he had seen this guy before. It might have been the Lihue courthouse, but it could have just as easily been the local L & L BBQ picnic tables.

"Well, as you can imagine, drawing those lines inland is going to destroy the real estate value along the entire coast." Cecil leaned back in his chair to where the front two legs were up off the saw dust covered floor.

"Maybe for the older structures, but as you must certainly know, the entire beachfront has already been zoned fifteen feet up."

Cecil let his chair fall forward forcefully and slammed his fist onto the table, scaring the brunette.

"Yeah? No shit. I hear these new lines are going in a full mile or until the terrain rises at least two hundred feet." He gently picked his fist up from the table. "Do you know what that's going to do to Kukui Wai'ale'ale?"

Now John recognized this guy. He was the Maui developer who had just magically received rezoning of a hundred acres of abandoned taro fields for a new high-end housing subdivision. Everyone knew it was a bad idea on so many levels. Whomever had chosen that combination of those Hawaiian words, Kukui Wai'ale'ale, didn't realize it translated to "oily nuts overflowing". Of course, that might turn out to be more accurate if the units eventually sold to suntan lotion lathered mainlanders who didn't realize they were surrounded by a swamp.

This Cecil character had just recently donated $400,000 to Hanalei School, Hanalei Fire Station, Hanalei Auditorium and to the Hanalei VFW luau building. The abandoned taro patches were an eyesore anyhow, according to the Kauai Land Use Board. That they might be, but several lawsuits by Hanalei residents were sure to hold it up for a while. Still, people were getting nervous. The multi-thousand unit Princeville resort, only three miles up the road, had snuck up on them back in the '80s. This new assault, by a foreign developer no less, on their rural lifestyle, couldn't be allowed.

John stood up, taking the brunette's hand in his.

"Look, Cecil. Personally, I don't give a damn about Kukui Wai'ale'ale. The mosquitoes are going to eat you up, anyhow. You know what I sell. My listings are already under the strictest rules. Beach mansions have that problem. Waterproof basements are not for the faint of heart. I suggest you re-evaluate your swamp land and go try your hand on Lana'i. I hear they want to pave it with wind turbines."

The brunette followed John outside to several cheers, mostly directed at the young lady.

Onolani watched all of this from the bar, sipping a guava juice that had somehow come in contact with a shot, or was it two, of rum. She knew exactly who Cecil from Maui was. Every hippie in town understood what he was all about. And it wasn't peace and love.

And it wasn't going to be solved at the moment anyhow, not on open-stage open-mic Karaoke night. Onolani soon saw the bottom of her glass and began to wonder who would go up on stage first.

That's when she noticed her hitchhiker, Pat, walk up there with a ukulele tucked under his arm. She caught her breath at the sight. His Aloha shirt was perhaps the most brilliantly colored one she had ever seen; he stood up so tall he almost touched the low ceiling, and most importantly, he was looking at her.

"Wahines and Kanes," he said in a booming voice, "Let me dedicate this first song to my new friend Onolani, sitting at the bar. A true angel."

seven

~~~

Trish was in the throes of a dream as the first light began sneaking onto the screened lanai of Hale Ha Ha O'Hanalei. The reds and oranges of pre-dawn wove themselves around the brightly colored throw pillows, bounced off the various bamboo finished furniture and finally penetrated her eyelids.

She was standing on a warm beach, barefoot but wearing a Chicago style parka and holding an old hand between both of hers. Her focus studied the withered hand, blotched with age spots and shaking slightly. Quite out of character, she was feeling incredibly sympathetic, almost lovingly so, as her eyes moved up to look. There, fading quickly into an increasing light was her old mailman from back home. He was smiling broadly as he gently withdrew his hand and disappeared.

Then, as dreams are apt to do, it changed and she found herself back in her old college dorm, having her toes licked. It was impossible to tell who was licking up and down and between her wiggling toes but very quickly it became too ticklish, and she opened her eyes.

Poi looked up from his ministrations and wagged his butt furiously back and forth, happy to have awoken someone to play with.

"Not what I was expecting..." Trish said, her voice hoarse with the remnants of her cold and the texture of too much rum.

Poi jumped down from the punee, ran over to the screen door leading outside, and then ran back to the punee. His untrimmed nails clicked on the wooden floor, but when his little butt wagged back and forth, his nails simply slid sideways. Trish knew she was tired, and probably a bit dampened in her senses, but that sideways movement of his nails against the wood sounded like crickets.

"I guess you need to go out," she said, holding her head against the pounding of a fresh but mild hangover.

The only thing going for Trish before dawn was that her body was still on a clock five hours earlier. She was quickly awake, as if she had slept until noon on a snowy Chicago weekend.

Standing up and moving toward the screen door to let Poi out, she immediately realized something was very different. The floor wasn't cold. In fact, it felt comfortably cool against her bare feet. Her next breath found plumeria hovering in the air, and then she heard the birds.

Light chirping songs quietly moved among the coconut trees outside as the sky continued brightening. Opening the door for Poi, she looked out from the second story landing and gasped. The high peaks behind Hanalei valley were already touched with the golden light of the morning sun.

Poi ran to the first papaya tree, lifted his leg for what seemed too short of a time, then ran directly to the box of towels just under the eaves of the roof. He grabbed one and looked back up the stairs to Trish.

The morning stillness had only a hint of ocean waves gently sliding along sand, the sound itself almost a whisper. Trish took another deep breath, holding onto the railing for support. That whisper was exotic, promising; perhaps even seductive.

"Wait a sec, Poi," she whispered. Onolani was no doubt still sleeping and the neighboring houses were still dark.

Trish walked back, found her as yet unopened luggage, rummaged around for her one-piece swimsuits, picked the dark blue one and paused. Should she change right out here? In the middle of the TV room?

Poi was now scratching at the screen door, anxious to get going. Trish quickly walked down the narrow hallway to see if Onolani was indeed asleep. All the side bedrooms were empty, but at the end of the hall, the house opened up into two very large suites. There, in the one to the left, she saw Onolani's bare feet sticking out from a hibiscus decorated blanket. Horribly disturbing sounds vibrated throughout her room. As there were no bears in Hawaii, she figured it was her sister's snoring.

Trish quickly walked past the empty bedrooms, the two bathrooms and back out onto the lanai, and found a view of the mountain peaks from a different punee bed. There, she stripped off her remaining mainland clothes, removed her hair tie and brazenly pulled up her one-piece swimsuit.

Her head still pounded slightly as she descended the stairs to Poi and the towels, but she felt a lot better than she had in a really, really long time.

~~~

David Lesperance, geologist in residence now, watched the sun just cresting the horizon from the end of the Hanalei pier. His flight had arrived early, direct into Lihue from Los Angeles. Hawaiian Airlines was firing on all cylinders, or turbines, as the case may be. His various pieces of luggage were first to the baggage carousel.

He had not expected so much to go right on a tropical island. His coffee at Auntie Lolo's Coffee & Cream turned out to be exactly what he ordered as well as perfectly warm. What he had expected was a good dose of eccentricity, and early morning Hanalei served it up in heaping doses.

Some half naked, gray hair hippie guy was out standing in a taro field silently playing an electric guitar. A uniformed fireman was riding his bicycle to work, with his pre-school kid perched on the handlebars. Outrageously colored roosters marched across the road, stopping the light traffic, their harem of hens following closely and a less organized trail of chicks bringing up the rear. Across from the coffee shop, middle aged women, decked out in the same pastels they sold, opened their dress shops. Early rising tourists beginning their daily adventure, still six time-zones ahead of everyone else, paused unusually long at the stop signs, reading the two dozen stickers adorning them.

Somewhere in the middle of those two extremes of efficiency and eccentricity were the fragrant flowers. Everywhere: in planter boxes, bordering parking areas, spilling out of every possible space flowers bloomed. Even the weeds alongside the road, tenaciously pushing aside concrete, asphalt or rocks, sparkled without any need of a pedigree.

But he was here to work. Before attending a planned meeting at some popular bar at 6 P.M. Dave wanted to do two quick surveys. This morning's would be a zodiac ride along the Hanalei bay, Wainiha bay and out toward Hanakāpī'ai beach. The afternoon would be a two hour helicopter tour completely around the island. Both were introductory tours to the lay of the land. The meeting tonight, though, would introduce him to the lay of the emotions on the subject.

He expected a lot of resistance to his project from any and all communities that were in low lying areas near the ocean. The current tsunami high water lines seemed, at first glance, based on historical run-ups of past events. Everyone at the USGS knew those historical marks were woefully inadequate for at least two reasons. Firstly, the history of such recordings went back less than 200 years in the Hawaiian Islands. Secondly, big tsunami, like the 2011 Japan event proved that some waves were simply too overwhelming to simply dismiss as rare or unusual. They had to be planned for as well. The Japanese fishing village of Riyoishi had built a 30 foot tall concrete wall. It was broken and topped, completely destroying the remote village for a second time in a century. A new approach to coastal living had to be considered.

Dave was of the personal opinion that reconstructions, like the one in Hilo, Hawaii, where the harbor waterfront was abandoned and turned into a park instead of more shops and homes, was the only viable option. Despite his personal opinions, though, he would let the science make the decision. He was only its faithful servant.

As he awaited his chartered ride on TR's Dolphin Zodiac Experience, the slight offshore breeze brought hints of a now abandoned beach fire, some seaweed and something sweet, perhaps

48

incense. Or it might be some kind of flower. In any case, as he caught the approach of a fast moving zodiac, he turned again for a moment toward the low slung community nestled behind palms and naupaka. It was a vast improvement over the way Santa Ana smelled.

~~~

Trish followed Poi, wagging butt and all, down Mahimahi Street until they found Weke Road. Poi turned left. After fifty yards or so, he turned right onto Kee Street. Two minutes after leaving Hale Ha Ha O'Hanalei Trish was at the beach, no longer following the little dog, but walking in something of a trance as she stepped out onto the wide expanse of sand.

Poi looked back at Trish to make sure she was OK for the moment. It appeared that she might just be, so he turned back toward the ocean and ran full speed at the approaching tiny waves. Just as his feet hit wet sand and mere moments from feeling the first surge of water, Poi jumped up and over the six inches of rushing water. His tiny legs were spread out in front, and trailing behind, as he soared over the first wave. Little ears flapped in the wind about as happily as his tongue was.

A second or so later he glided down lower, impacting into the approaching second wave, tumbled twice, felt for the bottom and turned to race back to the beach. To the uninitiated, his little yelps might have indicated distress. Onolani had briefed Trish, though, that this was the only voice he had to celebrate with. Despite Onolani's several attempts with dog whisperers and canine singing coaches, his vocal range was incapable of all but about two notes within one mid range octave.

Trish walked out farther until her toes began that wonderful sink into the warm, wet sand. There she simply stood still, letting her weight sink her a little lower as the little waves lapped at her ankles. She closed her eyes and let her head back just a little, breathing in as much of the ambiance as she could. This was, she had to admit, her first experience with the ocean. The Jersey shore had enticed her once, but the cold quickly put a stop to any thought of getting in the water there. And, since Lake Michigan didn't count despite the seagulls, this was all new. Wonderfully new.

She turned to watch Poi charge back up into the dry sand so he could get another good running start for his next flight. As she turned, she suddenly noticed the towering green mountain peaks surrounding the bay. It appeared to be an immense natural amphitheater, holding her there in the front row seating.

As far as she could see, perhaps a mile down the beach, there were maybe four people, all jogging. How could there not be a million people down here enjoying this? She glanced up at the sky, as she might there spy the good fortune that had just given her this winning lottery ticket. All she saw were deep dimensions of blue reflecting down into the crystal clear sea.

Poi looked to have gotten a little over his head on his last flight and was dog-paddling back toward Trish. She took a few steps toward him, paused when her swimsuit got wet, but then plunged in after the little guy.

Easily picking him up, she cradled him in her arms and walked a little deeper. A zodiac was leaving the pier to her right, but other than that, no boats marred the view.

"Poi, you crazy little dog," Trish said softly, hugging him. "How did I not get here a long time ago?"

The little dog flexed and twisted in her arms until he could reach up and lick away the tears on her cheeks.

eight

~~~

"Did you get it done?"

"Yes, sir. Pictures of him getting into the zodiac by himself at the pier."

"Anything else?"

"Yeah, I don't think it'll ..."

"Don't think! Just tell me!"

"We got some shots of him leaving his rental, no shirt, with a towel draped over his shoulder. Looks like your typical tourist on vacation, just like you asked."

"Good. What about the apartment?"

"We had a key, so no damage getting in. His laptop was secured well, so we couldn't get into it. But, we did find quite a bit of some kind of scientific stuff. I don't know what the hell it is, meters or something I guess."

"Any incriminating stuff? You know, lots of alcohol bottles, porn, women's underwear?"

The voice reporting to his boss paused at that question. Surveillance was one thing, but character assassination was going to be more expensive.

"No, sir. We'll keep watching him, though."

Cecil hung up the phone and sat back on his expansive Princeville lanai. The view out over Hanalei bay was spectacular. His binoculars could still pick up the zodiac as it made its way west. He scanned to the left, toward his yet undeveloped taro fields. Letting his mind wander for just a moment, he smiled. One day there would be beautiful mansions there, underground utilities, electric sport cars, spas, fine restaurants and most of all, no hippies!

The hippie lifestyle was for young, poor kids. Not rich, middle-age developers trying to bring rural Hawaii into the 21st century. Hippies were keeping Hanalei in their firm grasp. They weren't bad people, just anti-growth. Some people simply liked to live in treehouses and smoke pakalolo all the time.

He had tried the hippie thing once, when he was young and stupid, experimenting with all the trappings of that lifestyle on Maui. There was only one part, one person, he remembered fondly, but she was probably dead from an overdose or something by now, he figured. The only thing the hippies got right, Cecil concluded, was the free love thing. Everything else needed to be eliminated, paved over and forgotten.

A rooster howled obnoxiously below his balcony, disturbing his thoughts of improving the island all on his own.

Standing up to go inside and watch the news he spoke directly to the rooster below. "After Kukui Wai'ale'ale, the chickens must go."

~~~

Captain Tim Wheeler steered his glass bottom zodiac along the curve of Hanalei bay, watching his client closely. He knew what the California geologist was up to; everyone on the north shore did. Most of his neighbors were worried. He wasn't.

Change, as Tim knew, was a fighting word in this community. For most people here, deathly afraid of another Princeville resort event, anything that might upset the fragile balance between holding off growth and preserving what they cherished was evil. Perhaps, but Tim knew change wasn't always bad.

Change had brought him to Kauai. First, to Poipu on the south side where things had been difficult. Change relocated him again to Kapa'a where business never really took off, either. Finally, more change convinced him to try Hanalei, almost as a last option. It was going to *have* to work. The alternative to being his own boss, of owning his own business in the beautiful tropical islands of Hawaii was inconceivable.

Completely stressed out about his options he had wandered into the Tahiti Nui on his first night in Hanalei. It seemed the best thing to do. Avoiding another night of crunching numbers on a spreadsheet to calculate how long his retirement money would last might be therapeutic.

With several Mai Tai bombs working their way through his bloodstream, he sat at the bar, quietly watching the action all around. People of all types filtered in and out. Tourists, local men and women, Hollywood types of questionable fame, someone's young kids, a few hobos and backpackers from the Kalalau trail were there. Everyone was talking, everyone was enjoying themselves. Something about this bar, unlike any he had been in before, seemed to liven people up.

The band was excellent, working the friendlies in the crowd, laughing and inviting people to dance.

"I'm Chad Pa folks and we are *In Season*." He paused and grinned. "You know, *always ripe!*" The crowd all cheered as the band members left their instruments on stage for a break and immediately began accepting the free drinks being offered.

That's when he heard it.

The backpacker types, young, fit, tanned and happy to have survived, were talking next to him.

"I would have loved to get a ride back from Kalalau," one of them was saying.

"Helicopters won't land there anymore," another said. "Too expensive, anyhow."

"I saw some dilapidated zodiac picking up a few hikers, but it looked like a pirate ship. Four people got in with their packs and I swear it looked like it was sinking before it got back out into the waves."

The last one of the backpackers, who sat glassy eyed next to Tim, finally chimed in. She was perhaps the most beautiful girl he had seen since, well, ever. Except for the red eyes.

"If I could see all those beautiful little fishes while being carried back from Kalalau I would kiss the captain!"

Certainly, change was sometimes good! The next day, TR's Dolphin Zodiac Experience was born. Initially, though, it had only been the *Kalalau Glass Bottom Taxi*. The dolphin thing was something new.

"So, I gotta ask." Dave turned to Captain Tim. "What's up with all these bikini tops tied to the outside of your boat?"

Tim smiled. He told this story every day.

"I find them just floating out in the near waters almost every day. I picked them up at first, just like I would a plastic bottle. Those straps could get tangled around a turtle or something."

Dave laughed out loud. "Really? Where are they coming from?"

Tim smiled. "I guess all these tourist girls feel they don't need them here, and just throw them off."

Dave turned to immediately scan the beaches, but there was no one out sunbathing yet.

"So, why tie them to the sides then?"

"Funny story," Tim said. "It was an especially windy day, and I was getting soaked all the way back from Kalalau. Waves were splashing in and I was losing all the tops I had collected. I actually had to circle back around a few times and collect them again. So, I figured I would tie them to the boat. They ended up hanging over the sides."

Dave was still scanning the beaches for people throwing their bikini tops into the sea.

"Almost immediately after tying them off," Tim continued. "We got a pod of dolphins surrounding us. With the glass bottom, all my passengers could see them swimming underneath and then popping up on our bow. We had an escort all the way back to Ke'e beach!"

Dave almost believed him. "But seriously, you have hundreds tied to your boat. Are you really finding this many floating in the water?"

Tim steered toward shore a little closer since the water was deeper in this one particular area. Maybe his one paying passenger would see something he liked.

"No, but when word got out that the glass bottom zodiac taxi with the bikini tops tied to the side was attracting a dolphin escort on every trip … well, then these young Euro tourist women would donate theirs. You know, they want to be part of the mystique.

"People were booking rides to Kalalau just to ride both directions, just to see the dolphins, and in a lot of cases just to see the donations happen. My prices have risen every year and I can barely keep up with all the bookings."

Dave saw that he was serious. It made a thought cross his mind. Perhaps geology wasn't the only fascinating career one could choose. But, as he explored that idea, he couldn't find a way that rocks and topless women could be paired together as a business. Disappointed, but hopeful, he went back to scanning the coastline.

~~~

Trish and Poi were walking back up the stairs to Hale Ha Ha O'Hanalei after Poi had showed her how to rinse her feet in the concrete basin.

"Brilliant, Poi," Trish had said. The sun had warmed the basin water so much so that she had stood in there until Poi circled back around to get her.

"You must be hungry by now," Trish whispered, in case Onolani was still asleep. She didn't know what she would feed him, having given him the entire Ziplock bag of bacon strips last night.

She pushed the never-locked screen door open and tiptoed in, Poi running quietly ahead. It was quiet, but there on the floor, sitting in some kind of exotic yoga pose was Onolani. Her eyes were closed, her mouth silently speaking, her fingers curled up toward the same ceiling the incense was twisting toward.

Trish hadn't seen her sister meditate since she was a teenager. The colorful pareo, clinging loosely around her frame, moved easily with her deep breathes. Other than confirming Onolani had the aging issues of a someone a decade older, and that the pareo was all that she was wearing, she was surprised to see hints of an unbroken tan across her entire body.

Poi's tap dancing on the wooden floors prompted Onolani to open her eyes. She raised her hands up into the air happy to see the both of them.

"Aloha!" Her pareo slipped a little.

Trish caught her eye quickly and averted her gaze toward the coffee pot. "Good morning, Ono."

Onolani stood gracefully, considering how much unfolding she had to do, wrapped the day's new pareo a little tighter around her and walked up to Trish.

"A big, cosmic good morning hug to you!"

Trish, her back turned, tensed up thinking this might be some weird hippie greeting. She turned quickly in time to see it wasn't.

"Oh, yes!" Trish breathed with some relief. "Hugs back at you."

Onolani held on for a measurable amount of time after Trish was ready to let go, but Poi enjoyed it as he made another few circles around the both of them.

"I went down to the beach..." Trish said.

Onolani let her go and stood back. "Was it awesome?"

Trish didn't expect that word from someone her age, but it did fit the answer better than she would have expected.

"Yes, actually, awesome is a perfect word." Trish turned to pour a cup of coffee. "Why aren't there any people on the beach, though? Have there been shark attacks or medical wastes washing up or an oil spill, maybe..."

"No! No, Trish, none of that. Of course not!" Onolani was a bit horrified.

Turning to sit on the large bamboo padded chair, Trish continued. "Well, I don't get it Ono. That beach is spectacular; the mountains are so beautiful they made me cry. Why isn't the entire island down there?"

Onolani walked over to the punee and sat on its edge. Poi jumped up and lay down next to her hip.

"Why *isn't* the whole world here?" Onolani asked. "Birdman explained it to me." She glanced up to Trish just then. That name would need an explanation before she continued, or Trish would discount everything else that followed it.

"Birdman is an old squeeze of mine, long ago old, not old-old," Onolani laughed. "Got his name from the way he used to surf. He was the King of Tunnels back in the day. The way he dropped in on big waves was arms held high, then as he hit his bottom turn, they flapped down, then back up again. Sometimes three or four times. People used to think he was a bit goofy."

Trish nodded unconsciously at that.

"But," Onolani added. "He never fell off. Ever."

Trish smiled politely, working up the courage to not discount everything else her sister would say.

"Ever?" she asked.

"Ever!" Onolani folded her arms and looked in the direction of a spontaneous rooster squawk. "Kind of freaky actually. Some of the guys he surfed with thought he was some kind of reincarnated turtle, or fish or something.

"I knew better than that," Onolani said with a smirk. "He was *all* man."

Trish saw something just then in her sister. It moved right through her, like a shiver. Not a cold shiver. Not a scared shiver. It was a subtle vibration that seemed to move through her like a light breeze might do.

"He taught me how to hula, you know." Onolani looked up with sparkles bursting from her eyes. "Real Hawaiian hula, not some hippie love dance."

Trish caught the self depreciation, for her benefit, and smiled broadly at her sister.

"Ono... Onolani, there's nothing wrong with being a hippie. Not in my book, anyhow."

Poi barked once, on cue when such proclamations were made, and jumped off the punee, sliding and tapping his way across the wooden floor. Onolani giggled, stood up and bowed deeply.

"Come here, big boy!" Trish welcomed Poi at her feet. Bending down to pick up the little dog, she asked. "So, what did Birdman explain to you? About why the whole world isn't out there on that gorgeous beach?"

Onolani stood up again, tightened her pareo and walked over for more coffee.

"Contrast." Onolani stopped speaking and let the word hang in the air long enough to easily be defined as irritating.

"I know," she said, interrupting her own silence. "Birdman did the same thing to me, pausing like that, like I'm supposed to figure out what the hell he is talking about from just one word."

"I couldn't resist." Onolani laughed again. Trish finally noticed the pattern that had been knocking at her consciousness for the last two days now. It was her sister's easy laugh. Deeper than her natural voice it added a tone of interest to whatever subject entertained her. It was quite distinctive and now Trish could confirm that every time she had heard it that she had felt a tiny bit better herself.

"He said," Onolani continued. "People need contrast in their lives sometimes, to reassure themselves that they are doing what feels right to them." She twisted a little in a light stretch, then continued. "Most people that come to Hanalei do one of two things. They find confirmation that their comfortable life back 'home' is the best place for them and that Hanalei was a 'nice place to visit'. Most people fall into this category."

Trish set Poi down and turned for more coffee as well.

"But a few see the contrast, as Birdman used to tell me, like a big, loud cosmic slap-in-the-face wake-up call to change."

"That's gotta hurt," Trish said, trying to lighten up the conversation a little.

"Oh, it does. I can assure you it did. Birdman would tell you the same thing."

Trish turned with her coffee and leaned over onto the polished palm wood bar top. "What do you mean, hurt? Like how?"

"This place," Onolani said with a cautionary tone in her voice. "It can... hold you, maybe a little too tight. Birdman, myself, a dozen others I can think of, all gave up quite a bit to stay in this little slice..."

"...of heaven?" Trish guessed.

Onolani nodded. "We've got people calling it that, others paradise and such. Maybe it is; I don't honestly know. The analogy that works for me is that this place is a drug. A spiritual drug with no deadly side-effects." She took a long sip of coffee, then set her cup down and walked back to the punee. "It can make you feel real good while nothing gets done. Or it can inspire your soul to reach the heights it was designed to."

Trish let that sink in for several moments. "It sounds addictive."

"Yeah, and rehab never works." Onolani shrugged.

~~~

Pat was attempting to calm himself down. He had just discovered that yes, his new business was indeed outside the so-called "disaster-zone" reach of the current tsunami lines. By one foot.

The realtor hadn't told him how deep into the safe zone he was, nor had he asked. Upset at himself for such a lapse in research he had climbed up onto the roof to see if there was anything else he might have missed.

The view was spectacular. A fine carpet of swaying coconut palms spread out before him. The crescent beach of the bay could be seen from here arching out toward the sea. No buildings nearby were any higher than his one-story bar. From this vantage point the magic still worked. He climbed back down the ladder and went into his small office off the kitchen.

Pat consoled himself with the fact that prior to this week, there was no idea that new tsunami lines would even be considered. But, that wasn't much consolation. When he had signed the purchase agreement, it had not been quite the horrendous bet that it now appeared it might have been. New lines would certainly be inland and certainly include Tahiti Nui. Any improvements to the bar would have to pass by the new building codes and that could quickly get cost-prohibitive.

Other issues were impacting operations as well.

Besides the latest county fine to upgrade the sewer system, two employees had just taken their mandatory eight week maternity leave. Except one was actually on paternity leave. Eight weeks! The State of Hawaii was serious about babies. The kid would be in pre-school before the parents come back to work, Pat lamented to himself.

Receipts weren't as bad as he had thought, mostly because the rent on the land was so low. He had insisted on two more years of that rate with the seller, who owned the land, but after that it could potentially skyrocket. With only four tables and a woefully short bar run, there simply wasn't enough space to bring in more people and up the profits.

Tiki Man Pizza, behind the bar, was holding its own but sending little, if any, revenue back to the mother ship.

Drink prices were already approaching tourist-level so with half the patrons being local that was getting dangerous. Tahiti Nui might be the most famous bar on the island, but it wasn't immune to competition. A dozen cleaner, better decorated bars were all within walking distance.

The kitchen was bringing in a solid 45% of revenue and for a bar that was indicative of low drink sales. But, Pat noticed, bar sales were excellent considering they ran an average of thirty tabs a night. So, he reasoned, there was good potential cash flow; he just needed to divert more of it to the coffers and out of those good people's pockets.

He would start with t-shirts, despite the fact that t-shirts shops outnumbered banana plants in Hanalei. This was a branding issue. Tahiti Nui's best resource was its reputation. He had to start there. The fact that nicely dressed tourist ladies walked into such a place for a moderately priced lunch menu was amazing. Especially with the horrible signage, location right *on* the road and the fact that the building was actually a wooden ninety-five year old former home of a taro farmer. And it looked it. Yet, they filled the tables every day it wasn't raining.

T-shirts they would buy. They had already bought the mystique.

~~~

"What've you've got?"

"Good photos of your guy boarding Air Kauai for the helicopter tour."

"He's not 'my guy', he's a frickin' geologist about to..."

"With a young lady."

"No shit? Tell me more."

"We got two shots of them both together, but I..."

"But what? You killing me here!"

"I think it was just a regular tour, several other people boarded as well."

Cecil hung up, disgusted. This geologist was behaving like he was actually on a government paid job. So far, there was no evidence they could use against him, nothing to discredit him, his reputation or whatever results he came up with.

But the young lady on the helicopter... now, that gave him an idea.

nine

~~~

There was a gentle knock at the screen door as it opened slowly.

"Aloha..." someone whispered. "Onolani?"

Poi ran over to the door apparently already knowing whomever it was would be welcome. No bark marred the morning's quiet.

Trish turned to see a flower decorated head of glimmering black hair enter, framing a most elegant smile within a beautifully brown background.

"Kainalu!" Onolani almost sang. "Aloha kakahiaka."

Both women walked up to each other slowly, measuring their steps almost as if in dance, and hugged each other tightly.

"It is another beautiful morning," Onolani said softly, her head still on her friend's shoulder.

"Yes, oh yes," Kainalu said. She pulled back from the embrace and added, "So, we shall be beautiful with it then."

Onolani nodded without saying anything. Her mood had changed immediately upon her friend's arrival. The seriousness of their earlier discussion about the addictive nature of a spiritual lifestyle had disappeared immediately upon getting another fix.

"You must meet my sister." Onolani beamed. "Trish is here to worship with us today, at Ke'e beach."

Kainalu turned to Trish and held her arms out for a hug. Trish moved a little uneasily into the gregarious woman's arms, looking over Kainalu's hair flowers and shoulder at Onolani.

Onolani smiled and nodded lightly, but ignored Trish's uneasiness as something she would eventually shed with time.

"So, so wonderful to meet you, Trish." Kainalu said softly. "Welcome to Hanalei."

Trish stood back a step and smiled at the generous greeting, one of which would have been quite rare back in Chicago. "Thank you, I'm really enjoying myself so far."

Kainalu stood back now, next to Onolani. Trish noticed each of their hands come together in supplication.

"Ah, Trish," Kainalu said, tilting her head slightly to one side as she studied the newcomer. "You too have your sister's aura surrounding you." She turned to Onolani who nodded her agreement. Turning back to Trish, she bowed slightly, raising her pressed hands to meet her forehead. "Our 'aina, our land," she added in translation. "Will greet and embrace you today as one who can appreciate her magnificence."

"Thank you," Trish said, unable to find equivalent words to respond to such a proclamation. "Very much."

Kainalu smiled intently at Trish for the briefest of moments, then said quickly. "Hurry now, girls, we must beat all those tourists if we want a good parking spot."

Poi got the message and ran toward the door. Kainalu followed him, opening the screen for the dog as he scampered directly to the towel box.

Trish turned to Onolani, not intending to let her escape without some interpretation of their upcoming adventure.

"What's this about worship?"

Onolani, ever patient in her sister's education, predicted, "You can call it sightseeing today, if you like. Someday, though, you will come to acknowledge it was really worship."

~~~

The ride out to Ke'e beach, in Kainalu's ancient Dodge Caravan took only fifteen minutes. Yet Trish felt as if she had traversed hundreds of years as she moved deeper into the rural landscape of Kauai's north shore.

Most amazing to this city girl was the lack of any homes, roads or any touch of humanity on the ridges and rising land of the mountains. The views there must be glorious, she thought.

The entire ride crossed several one lane bridges, passed old wooden structures people still obviously lived in and glided past empty beaches. It appeared that there weren't even people in the water, as all she could see were sparkling bits of sun dancing quite happily alone on the blue water.

Finally, she saw several newer homes on the ocean side, perched ridiculously high atop long alien legs. If a big wave was coming they might simply walk away from danger.

"That," Onolani told Trish. "Is what happened the last time new tsunami information made it into the building code. Now, everyone's gotta be fifteen feet up."

"Auwe," Kainalu lamented. "But at least they got a shady place to park their trucks."

Onolani laughed so much, in her signature deeper tones, that Trish couldn't resist joining in a little.

"Kainalu, honey," Onolani said. "You are my teacher in so many, many ways. And, comedy is one of them!"

"No, Onolani," Kainalu said humbly. "You are *my* teacher, Obiwan. But you still need to find your light saber."

"Trish," Kainalu continued. "That's where I was born, there to the right."

Trish saw only a few scraggly trees trying to compete against a few ancient coconut palms.

"Where?"

"Taylor Camp, honey. A bunch of wonderful people made a go of it here. A long time ago. But that's where I grew up, on that beach."

Onolani was looking as well, turning to follow it as they passed. "You're so lucky, Kainalu."

"Blessed," Kainalu corrected.

They soon ran out of pavement and the Dodge moved easily into the twenty space parking area at Ke'e Beach Park, claiming one of the eighteen or so open spots.

"Good, we beat the crowd," Kainalu sang out.

Trish looked at her watch, first noticing that it was kind of silly that she was still wearing one, and secondly that it was 8:20 A.M.

"Is Poi OK without a leash... ?" Trish asked as the little dog rocketed out of the side door and churned his tiny legs across the pavement, through the sand and toward the calm lagoon.

"Watch this," Onolani said, steering Trish quickly to where she could see the lagoon clearly. "He's going to..."

Kailani and Onolani started laughing before Onolani could even finish her statement. Trish had seen it before but this launch from the water's edge, pushing off from the sandstone slabs there, put Poi higher than ever above the mirrored surface.

They could hear his little yelps as he soared again, legs outstretched and his back arched in flight. He was still yelping as he hit the water, skipped twice and submerged.

"How did you teach him to do that?" Trish asked.

"Oh, honey. He learned that one all by himself. I've never seen any dog get so much air as Poi does."

"It's like he was a rabbit in his past life, or something," Trish joked.

"Or perhaps a bird," Kainalu said, smiling, confident in her guess.

They walked past the new lifeguard stand, looking a bit like a parked alien spaceship, and out onto the cool sand. Poi was back up into the shallowest waters, where his short feet could reach, yelping and shaking the water off his back.

Trish was staring back at the parking lot and was going to ask a question about car break-ins and robberies. As she turned back to speak she found Onolani and Kainalu swapping their pareos and necklaces in some kind of silent beach ceremony. She stared, enthralled with surprise, as the two almost middle aged women slowly wrapped the other's pareo around their unbroken tans.

Poi made his way back up the beach, turned and with a loud yelp that no doubt signaled a desire for attention, began another take off run toward the water. He got some.

Trish found herself surrounded, no, she thought, immersed in a world she couldn't have imagined. Sure, she understood Hawaii had beautiful mountains, clear blue oceans and warm sand. Yet she also found that among those known treasures existed fantastic creatures, human and otherwise, that seemed to celebrate their good fortune in strange, and admittedly wonderful ways.

On one side of her was a flying dog leaping into the ocean and on the other, two colorfully decorated hippie women bowing to each other in the middle of a public beach. Stranger yet, the half dozen people spread across the expansive cove didn't seem to notice, much less care. Most, Trish soon found, were intent on exploring their own good fortune at being there.

Content now to simply sit and observe, she watched as Onolani and Kainalu now held hands and walked together into the lagoon. Their other arms were raised high, and soon she heard them singing softly, happily.

Poi, finally exhausted from his flying and swimming walked over and sat next to Trish, looking out to where the ladies were now submerging themselves. He looked over to Trish, caught her attention and turned his head back to the sea, closing his eyes.

Trish watched the little dog closely, was he really... meditating? After a minute, she thought he must be indeed, except that every few moments he licked the air with his little tongue. No doubt a trick he had learned from the gecko, he sat perfectly still otherwise, eyes closed.

Perhaps it was his rare full-color vision that often forced him to shut out the overwhelming. The ocean just outside of the reef was cobalt and snow white, mixing together in a jumble of motion that hypnotized any that might stare. The sky above it was impossibly clear, sporting some kind of crisp-blue she had never seen before. Turning to her left, the marching jungle greens and textures only paused when they reached the water's edge, spilling down from the mountains and ridges above. Even the sand she sat on was multi-colored.

Poi still had his eyes closed, but he didn't really appear to be trying to shut anything out. Remarkably, she thought, he looked to be letting something else in. She tried it as well, gently letting her eyes, and her mind, relax. Knowing all of those wonderful visuals were just there, outside her eyelids, she found she could now experience better the subtle sounds all around them. Poi, she laughed quietly... Zen master.

Almost imperceptibly, she picked up her sister and her friend's sweet voices, no doubt still worshiping with song. The gentle movement of water onto soft sand, balanced some distance out by deep undulations of a great ocean, didn't overwhelm its song. Next to her, she could hear the slow breaths of Poi, and his occasional licking of the air. Far back along the Kalalau trail, which entered into the parking lot, she heard laughter. The light morning tradewinds were tickling the palm branches. It seemed as if the entire place was smiling - happy to have their company.

Her own breath was slowing; her own heart was beating rhythmically, trying to match this cheerful pulse of nature. Beauty was all around her, and it welcomed her as one of its own. She felt beautiful here, she felt as if now, finally, she had always been beautiful.

The sun against her warming skin was deepening its message, now clear and distinct, a message she was quickly enlightening to: our souls feed on nature's beauty, and just as voraciously, nature feeds on ours.

~~~

She wasn't quite sure how much time had passed. The sounds caressing her ears soon included a boat engine, and the spell quickly began dissolving. Right before she opened her eyes, she found her tongue was out, licking the air. That realization completed the move out of the trance. She turned quickly toward Poi to see if he was still meditating. He was looking at her, grinning in that unique ways dogs do when they see people imitate them.

A bright blue zodiac rounded the corner from the Na Pali coast cliffs and slowed as it entered Ke'e's quiet lagoon. Poi immediately ran over to greet the travelers, wagging his little butt so furiously it was difficult for him to move as quickly as he wanted to.

As soon as the bow slid up and stopped on the sand, Trish noticed some very exhausted backpackers climb out. Two of them literally poured themselves over the side, one of them actually kissing the ground. They looked so sunburned they glowed. Two others, young blondes without any backpacks waved at the captain and stepped out, topless.

Trish began to wonder if there might be a local regulation prohibiting women from covering their breasts. Onolani and Kainalu, were making their way over to the zodiac just as Poi, on his third try at leaping, made it inside.

Onolani turned toward her and waved her over.

"Captain Wheeler," Trish heard her sister saying. "Looks like another successful rescue." She was looking at the two beleaguered backpackers slowly move up and off the beach into the shade of the parking lot. Turning back to the zodiac and reaching down to the gunwales, picking up a handful of colorful bikini tops, she added, "And, some more contributions?"

The two topless blondes were splashing water at each other in the shallows, laughing and screaming like kids.

"Yep," Captain Tim Wheeler said. "All these hanging off the sides are probably hurting my gas mileage..." He paused as Trish walked up. "Aloha," he waved. "Ono, tell me who your friend is."

Onolani, Kainalu and Poi all turned toward Trish.

"This is my dear sister from far away."

Captain Tim saluted. He reached down and picked up little Poi, stroking his ears as he looked around.

"Well, I don't see anyone wanting a ride into Kalalau. I've got a pickup there at one o'clock. How about you ladies go for a ride with me?"

Poi yelped and wiggled in Tim's arms.

"Yeah, yeah, you, too, Poi," Captain Tim laughed.

Onolani looked to everyone, trying to gather their thoughts.

"What time would we be back?"

Captain Tim shrugged. "Difficult to tell. Could be four o'clock, could be dark."

Kainalu spoke up. "We've got the Hui meeting again tonight, with the geologist."

"Oh, yeah? I just gave that guy a ride yesterday."

Poi squirmed out of his arms quickly, intent on sniffing every nook and cranny of the boat floor.

"What's he like?" Onolani asked.

"Nice enough, but he didn't discuss much. Asked a few questions about the taxi business. I got the impression he wasn't too keen on jumping to any conclusions. But..."

The ladies waited as the pause lengthened into a baited prompt.

"But what?" Kainalu asked.

"Well, he was quite interested in how I got all these bikini tops tied to my boat."

"Ha!" Onolani scoffed. "Well then, we know he's breathing." She wrapped her pareo around a little tighter, digging her toes unconsciously into the sand. "We can't miss the meeting. Maybe another time?"

"Sure, ladies. Anytime." Captain Tim climbed out of his zodiac. "Where is this meeting tonight, Tahiti Nui again?"

Onolani nodded.

"Well, maybe I'll show up," Captain Tim said. "I don't go to bars often, but when I do, I go to Tahiti Nui."

~~~

"Is she on board?"

"Yes, sir. She has his address and should be knocking on his door any..."

"Is she dressed as I suggested?"

"Short skirt," the voice reporting to his boss enumerated. "Tube top - one size too small, long ear rings, sandals and..."

"Is she attractive? You know, slim, busty, big smile?"

There was a pause on the line, and Cecil looked quickly at his cell phone to see if he had lost signal yet again. He had not.

"Well? Is she... delicious?"

"Yes, sir. She's a professional."

"And the photographers are in place?"

"Right behind ---"

This time Cecil heard the connection click closed. The road was diving sharply alongside a cliff as they entered the valley. Another change this place needed was far more cell towers.

He was making his way to Hanalei for the Hui meeting, but not until he had his driver stop at the Kukui Wai'ale'ale site. The short black Mercedes limo crossed the old wooden bridge spanning the Hanalei

River and turned left, into the expansive Hanalei valley. All the other traffic, what there was of it, turned right toward town.

"Stop right here," Cecil commanded the driver. It was amazing what a buck above minimum wage could buy you these days. You just had to find the right kind of people. Like those living in their cars at the beach parks, or older down-on-their-luck guys without any local family, or both. Both was better.

"Yes, sir," the driver said, trying to sound like a professional, but biting his tongue against complaining, just hoping he got paid this week. The last guy that had complained about late pay was back living at the beach park. Putting the Mercedes into park, he looked around but didn't see any ripe fruit he might stash for a midnight snack.

Cecil stood alone out in front of his limo. The stench from the rotting vegetation floating in his abandoned taro fields was more than he could handle. A silk handkerchief held to his face managed to shield him from reality while he daydreamed about glory.

The main road would be a full two lanes, with marked bike paths on either side, flanked of course by wide sidewalks. It would curve seductively in thirty degree arcs, forgetting forever its straight and skinny, one lane mud and rock ancestry. Retro light poles would mark the spaces along both sides with soft but effective lighting, allowing those fortunate enough to live here a gentle glow in which to walk at night. Shops would greet those eager to explore the wonders of retail, and fine dining those wanting to spend lavishly on foreign foods. A wine cabaret would tickle the very air with piano and fine glassware toasting the genius behind it all, behind such an audaciously progressive new beginning for Hanalei, for the north shore and for Kauai.

Cecil watched as the last light of day slid slowly up to the very top of the great peaks watching over it all. The feeling that they might be mocking him was quickly dismissed as superstition. Surely, the very mountain his magnificent development would be named after would appreciate a better use of the neglected lands at her very feet. Surely. He turned and marched back to the dust covered limo.

"Let's go," Cecil demanded of his driver. He looked at the poorly shaven hobo he had hired, and knew it was time to dock his pay fifty cents an hour. Experience had taught him years ago that if he kept their self esteem low they would work for him as long as he needed them. Desperation, especially in the middle of a vast ocean with few jobs for men like these, kept his labor costs low. More importantly, it put sufficiently enough distance between Cecil and those in his employ to ensure his illusion of superiority.

The driver, having made a few bad decisions in life after the Army, turned in his seat so that he might back up without getting them stuck in the mud. He grimaced a little when he heard the stolen soup crackers crush inside his pocket.

~~~

The employees of Tahiti Nui were having a completely different experience with their new boss. After the two dollar an hour raise was announced, Pat had insisted they all take ukulele lessons, if they didn't already know at least ten songs. He would hire the tutors to come to their homes, the beach or even the bar.

Their so-called "family meeting" included the cook, the two bartenders, the waiter/greeter and the waitress, and Pat. Everyone sat out on the open lanai. The three patrons inside were properly supplied with two free drinks to keep them occupied during the meeting.

"We have a new logo here at this honorable establishment," Pat told them right before the setup for the Hui meeting began. He held up a new XXX Large T-shirt he had custom made in Kapa'a that afternoon.

Everyone read it slowly, out loud.

"Securing the Peace...

"... with ukuleles...

"and Mai Tai's?"

Pat grinned broadly. They loved it, but he might have to explain it anyhow. "You've got the Mai Tai thing down real good, and pretty soon we'll all be playing ukulele like pros."

Kala, the young Chinese-Hawaiian girl who had just started waitressing on her 21st birthday, raised her hand.

"Yes, Miss Lau," Pat pointed at her.

"What's it mean, *Securing the Peace?*"

"Good question, Kala." That very morning Pat had asked her twice if her name really was Kala Lau, but when she explained she had been born on a zodiac racing out of the Na Pali coast one stormy evening, he knew he would forever remember it.

"I worked for the government a long time," Pat explained. "I saw the world as one big, screwed up mess. I saw fortunes spent on new ways to kill each other and bigger fortunes spent on ways to keep that from happening. Music, especially this fine invention right here..." He held up his four string acoustic marvel. "... is the foundation of world peace!" Pat smiled at the slight exaggeration but added what he truly did believe. "If everybody in the world played ukulele there would be no defense industry."

The five employees stared at him, silently composing a picture of this wealthy, otherworldly weapons specialist adopting the one thing they understood implicitly: music, and especially the ukulele. It took a moment, maybe three, but suddenly it clicked in their minds simultaneously. They all stood up and clapped.

~~~

Dave had just stepped out of his small apartment's shower, amazed that someone had built one so small. He wrapped the plush towel he had brought with him from Santa Ana around his waist. He traveled enough to know the provided linen was never up to his standard.

The steamed up mirror put a slight mystery to the inevitable question all naked men asked themselves. Do I still look amazing? Dave nodded yes, but knocked on the wooden counter twice for good luck.

The sound reverberated loudly in the small room. Dave stood back and looked at the counter. He tapped it again. This time it was what he expected, a nice resounding confirmation that pressed board held up the sink. Then he heard two taps again.

It was the door.

Quickly, he untied the towel, threw it over his bare shoulder and slipped on his surf shorts. Barefoot he went to the door, just as they knocked again.

"Mister Lesperance! I have a very important message for you."

Dave leaned his head against the wall, despondent that temptation was once again presenting itself, at work. She sounded young or beautiful.

"Please, sir. I have a message from your office."

Immediately, hearing "your office" Dave went over in his mind the all important communication checklist.

Had he checked his email? Yes, only a few moments before his shower.

Did his cell phone show any missed calls? No.

Was the apartment phone message light blinking? There wasn't a light at all on the apartment phone.

Were there any dead carrier pigeons outside his door? He paused, knowing he would have to open the door for that one.

Slowly, he opened the hollow wooden door. Damn, he muttered to himself. She was both young *and* beautiful.

Her eyes looked him over and glittered in the fading afternoon light. "I have a message for you. Can I come in?"

"I'm not expecting any messages," Dave insisted, keeping the door partially closed. "Who are you? Do you have any identification?"

The eyes that had glittered only a moment before rolled a bit beneath gorgeous raised eyebrows. She reached into her purse. A second later, she slipped her hand through the open space holding a pair of sheer blue panties.

"Do I need any more introduction, Mister Lesperance?"

"Oh, Lord!"

Dave pushed her hand back outside, inadvertently touching the sheer fabric, almost panicking at the delicious feeling. He closed the door, locked the bolt and pulled the flimsy curtain tighter to the side of the window next to the door.

"Go away, please!" Dave shouted. "I'm here on government business. I'm a federal employee. Your intentions are felonious!"

Breathing hard, for several reasons, Dave leaned with all his weight against the door, half expecting the sex-crazed woman to fight her way in. Visions of her assaulted his mind. Her and perhaps a girlfriend or two holding him down and rubbing papaya lotion all over him... Wait. That was a dream from last week.

Anyhow, after a couple of minutes, he figured she had left. He peeked out from behind the curtain. She was gone. Cautiously, still subconsciously expecting a group of geology groupies to rush the open door, he looked around outside. The courtyard was empty, except for six or seven wild chickens.

That's when he noticed them. The sheer blue panties were hanging on the outside door knob. Quickly, he retrieved them, shut the door and locked the bolt. Leaning against the closed door, he took a long, deep breath, clutching the sheer exquisiteness.

The universe did indeed reward those who fought the good fight.

~~~

Birdman had on his best aloha shirt, black cotton docker shorts and the cleanest slippers he could find. He was early enough getting to Tahiti Nui that an open bar stool had his name on it. Literally. He had secretly carved his initials in all of them. B.M.

John Steinmiller was sitting with his latest student, a raven hair Canadian nurse only one or two steps away from getting her Stand Up Paddling Certificate of Completion. She was in town for another eight days, and as John assured her, grasping her wonderfully strong hands, she would most certainly complete the entire training. Last night, swimming at the bay, under the nearly full moon, she had demonstrated an amazing ability to hold her breath longer than John could still.

Pat was strumming the chorus to *Hanalei Moon* while greeting everyone showing up for the Hui meeting. He was getting quite good at playing the ukulele, singing and gently pushing insistent chickens off the lanai with his feet. He felt a little guilty about chasing off the birds. They had their best aloha colors on as well.

Onolani, Kainalu and Trish arrived just ahead of Dave, their two cars pulling into the dirt lot and actually parking next to each other. It was the typical contrast everyone on the island was familiar with. The clean cars had to be rentals. Kainalu's old Dodge was clean on the inside only, but the red dirt insisted on decorating the outside.

"Hey, is that the guy?" Trish whispered. Their windows were still down.

Onolani looked over at the business-man haircut, the tailored blue shirt and the briefcase. He glanced over at them, then quickly avoided eye contact.

"Yep, that's him."

Kainalu grabbed Onolani's hand quickly. "Should we jump him?"

Trish almost said something, like "are you kidding?" but Kainalu started laughing before she could.

"Nah," Onolani said, playing along. "They'll just send two of them next time."

They followed the geologist into the bar, filling in the vacuum where everyone moved aside as he entered. Trish could tell it wasn't so much a sign of respect but more akin to avoiding someone with the plague.

~~~

Captain Tim found the last remaining parking spot at Tahiti Nui, which was unusual. There were always several spots to park there. That was part of the mystique; Tahiti Nui was welcoming before you even left your car.

Good luck had been his First Mate for a while now. Or it could have been that Captain Tim had inherited the title *the Most Interesting Man on Kauai*.

Roosters stopped their crowing when he walked among them. Papayas quickened their ripening so that he might stop to pick them. Coconuts refused to fall in his presence, out of respect.

As he approached the steps to the bar, all the chickens stopped their incessant pecking and held their heads high. Pat noticed this as well, somehow automatically wanting to offer the distinguished Captain a free drink.

"Thank you, my good man," Captain Tim graciously replied, accepting the Dos Equis beer. "I hear you are the new proprietor of this venerable establishment."

"Why, yes, I am." Pat turned quickly to retrieve something from behind the bar, almost spilling Birdman's third drink. "Perhaps, sir, you would like one of our new t-shirts."

Captain Tim politely brushed it away. "No. Thank you. I don't often wear t-shirts, but when I do, they're wet and I'm entered into a contest."

Pat's trance was broken with that visual. He nodded and walked through the standing room only crowd and up onto the stage.

"Ladies and gentlemen," Pat stood a few feet away from the microphone, his booming voice needing little amplification. The bar was still buzzing, though. Dave was standing quietly against one wall, his briefcase held tightly against his chest, to block bullets or spears if necessary.

Pat tapped obnoxiously on the mic now, but no one got the hint. The crowd's noise was increasing. Captain Tim suddenly appeared with a vibrantly colored rooster, held it up to the microphone and squeezed.

In a town where roosters were generally ignored out of habit, this one's incredible pitch and delivery demanded everyone's attention. The bar immediately went silent.

Captain Tim turned and handed the proud bird to Pat. "Learn to use your local resources," he said and walked off stage into a small group of adoring backpackers, still grateful for their recent rescues.

"Ladies and gentlemen," Pat repeated. "Tonight, we are grateful to have the man everyone's been talking about for..."

"Grateful?" someone shouted from the crowd.

Pat stopped and held up his hands. "Yes, grateful. From what I understand Honolulu rarely gives anyone on Kauai a chance to comment on anything." A few murmurs among the tables confirmed that well known fact. "So, I am pleased to introduce Dr. Dave Lesperance, PhD of Geology from Santa Ana, California He has been commissioned to survey our fine island and determine whether any changes to our tsunami inundation maps are required."

The bar was silent, everyone working hard at suppressing a boo. Innate tropical politeness was winning. Barely.

"Let's hope we don't need any," Pat said, then stepped off the stage.

Dave pushed off the wall, checked his briefcase for any damage, found no bullet holes or spearheads, and took the stage. Nervously, he pulled his reading glasses from behind his pocket protector, slipped them on, missed his right ear, and got them on the second try.

"My name is Dr. Dave Lesperance..."

"Yeah, we got that already!" Laughter erupted from the crowd after the shout.

"Go back to California!"

"We don't need no stinkin' maps!"

"...updated maps!"

"Why do you want to destroy us?"

Dave stood frozen, aghast at the reception. He had been to hundreds of meetings with angry residents in various neighborhoods all over California, but none had been this hostile.

Suddenly, Captain Tim showed up on stage again with another colorful rooster. He gently pushed Dave to the side, taking the microphone.

"Hey! What?" Captain Tim was staring at the crowd with a withering gaze everyone recognized as "supreme stink eye".

The shouting quickly subsided.

"Where's the aloha here folks?" Captain Tim scolded. "I saw it when I walked in, when I saw the faces of my most excellent Hanalei neighbors." The crowd was respectfully silent. "Kimo, I see you there in the back. You know better than anyone here about newcomers, you're from Molokai only last week. And, you, Auntie. I heard you lost your prize chickens in the '64 tsunami, yes?"

Everyone turned to Auntie Lois, who was nodding.

Captain Tim looked over toward the bar. Birdman was giving him a double thumbs up. "This guy is only doing his job, and that is to protect us, despite the fact that most of us do business and live in what we already know is a flood zone." He continued to stare down the entire crowd for a full thirty seconds more, before walking one step to the side. Quickly, he returned, holding the bird up to the mic.

"Don't make me use the chicken!" He squeezed the bird anyhow, prompting another amplified crow that bounced off the old wooden walls several times. Finally exiting the stage, Captain Tim gently set the bird onto the bar and walked outside the bar to the open lanai, presumably to accept the accolades of the stars and moon.

Dave moved back up the microphone, took a deep breath that everyone could hear, and wiped a line of sweat from his brow. "Look, folks, I am simply doing a survey. I'm only assessing your existing shoreline and comparing that with updated USGS predictions about wave run-up.

"Historically, we have only a couple of hundred years of data in the Hawaiian Islands. In that short period of geologic time, you've had four fatal tsunami events. As most of you know, the entire Pacific Rim is firing off earthquakes on a daily basis. Most of them send tiny tsunami your way, ones we don't even alert you to.

"Added to that already dangerous situation is the fact that four hundred miles to your southeast sits the world's most active rift zone - on the Big Island. In my opinion, your biggest threat lies there, with a locally generated tsunami."

Dave was getting into his lecture groove; he set the briefcase down on the stage and started moving his hands in emphasis.

"The Japan event was as horrific as it was to them because that earthquake was among other things, generated only a few dozen miles offshore. If the southwest flank of the Big Island shakes off a big one, you've got about seventy-five minutes before the first wave arrives here.

"And, of course, you know, there's never just one wave. Usually the third or fourth is the largest. Banking on that is futile though, since reporting stations can quickly go offline in a big event. You could have a secondary quake even bigger than the first. That generates yet another sequence of waves. You could get pummeled for dozens of hours."

The crowd quietly listened, like they would to the news of an approaching massive tropical hurricane. Fear was a rare emotion in paradise, so when it was put on display, people paid close attention.

"My point is this: you cannot rely on sirens to always alert you to flee, or small planes to fly the coastline with loud speakers. You cannot build your entire fortunes, your lives, in the middle of a susceptible natural disaster zone without taking every perceivable precaution.

"Lastly, tsunami is a Japanese word that translates to "harbor wave". These types of energy pulses will focus more dramatically, pile higher if you will, in the increasingly confined areas of harbors. And bays."

Dave looked out the windows, hoping he might see the expansive Hanalei bay, but couldn't. The effect was not lost on the crowd.

"You've got a wonderful blessing here in Hanalei. A natural amphitheater of mountains surrounding a gorgeous bay. Unfortunately, that kind of natural geography accentuates a wave.

"I'm going to keep to the strictest scientific analysis in making my recommendations. No politics. I'm not here to ruin anyone's business or livelihood."

Pat brought over a draft in an icy mug. Dave took two quick chugs and it was gone.

"OK, I can take a few questions, now."

Cecil made his way forward in the crowd, waving his hand up high.

"Yeah, I've got a couple."

"Yes, you in the black shirt, sir."

"It's purple," Cecil corrected. "Look here, Mr. Lesperance..."

"It's Doctor Lesperance," Pat yelled to the delight of the crowd.

"Whatever," Cecil said. "What gives you the right to come here, from California no less, and tell us where to draw our new tsunami lines?"

Dave had expected that question, but not necessarily first.

"I applied for the job over two years ago. The Hawaii Civil Defense office awarded it to me a week ago. Next question."

Cecil paused. Two years ago? He had only purchased the taro fields for Kukui Wai'ale'ale eighteen months ago.

"Wait," Cecil said. "Two years ago? Precisely when did the bid post?"

There were no other hands up, no other questions. Dave reached down to pick up his briefcase. In a moment he was re-reading the original bid posting. "Yes, two years ago. Today actually. Two years ago today." He looked out to the crowd for hands.

Cecil had a host of inflammatory questions ready to fire off at the geologist. But this news was devastating. He had thought his $100,000 an acre purchase was the steal of the century. Now he smelled a dead mongoose. This was looking like some kind of local conspiracy that began with the savvy Hikaguchisan family he had bought the land from. No doubt they must have been in cahoots with the Kauai Land Use Board. The local rezoning people must certainly have known of this inevitable redrawing of tsunami lines, they had to have seen the bid - every government office in the state would have had it posted. They had required him to put forth community redevelopment money and for what? Land that was certainly going to be condemned for all time as a tsunami flood zone!

Cecil turned for the door, weaving through the crowd rudely, disgusted with his lack of intel about the workings of Kauai politics, disgusted with what suddenly appeared to be a big scam. As he heard questions from the crowd behind him, as he looked up toward those peaks above the valley, he felt the mountains mocking him again. The old real estate joke would now change from "got some swampland in Florida to sell you" to "got some taro fields in Hanalei…"

~~~

Geology, tsunami maps and their inherent lack of danceable music can only go on for so long. Pat signaled to Dave to cut the question and answer session short by yelling out to the entire bar "FREE DRINKS!"

The important stuff had already been covered, anyhow. Dave was answering questions now about the different kinds of lava. Having just explained the difference between a'a and pahoehoe and looking for another question Pat had been forced to act.

The tables and chairs got stacked outside again just as *Island Fresh* got the crowd to their feet. Onolani rescued every tourist from their rapidly shrinking pool of shyness and danced with each and every one of them like a wild woman. Kainalu found Kimo from Molokai and despite the tempo of the music, they slow-danced the rest of the evening. Trish simply moved into the middle of it all and crowd danced.

Dave hugged the bar, getting a few quick pints in him. He had survived and his briefcase had no puncture wounds. It had actually been enjoyable after Captain Tim, now dancing on the bar itself with four backpackers, had stepped in. As the third pint appeared in front of him, someone pressed softly into his left side and whispered hotly into his ear.

"I'm going to need my panties back soon."

Dave turned quickly to find the same young *and* beautiful girl that had thrust her hand inside his door. Emboldened with drink and confidence, especially after having spoken in public, he felt good enough now to fend her off.

"Why is that?" Dave asked, secretly reaching into his right pocket to insure the sheer blue fabric was still there.

"Because I don't have any on right now."

Dave couldn't help but glance down. Her dress was long but the slit up the side must have reached her ribs. He recognized her perfume as something so deliciously intoxicating that his beer no longer seemed important.

"That's a nice smell... I mean your perfume..."

"I call it *Unavoidable*." She stealthily slipped her hand up to his topmost button, released it, and moved to the next lower one. "It's far too hot in here. A man must breathe, yes?"

Dave knew a setup when he was in the middle of one, but he figured he could enjoy it for a few more seconds before running.

Avoiding her eyes seemed key to survival. As he glanced away again he noticed a very curious local lady watching them both. She sat by herself across the bar and was dressed in many yards of fabric, so expansive was her beauty. Dave noticed her fingers tapping to the music.

He took one long, last gaze at the professional lady, took one more long inhale of *Unavoidable*, memorized her curves beneath the dress and ran.

"Gotta go, honey!"

"What?"

Dave made a beeline to the expansively beautiful woman sitting alone, picked her hand up off the bar and looked into her surprised eyes.

"Please," he said with wide eyes. "Protect me from that skinny winch and dance with me now!"

~~~

By midnight Pat knew he had made a sound financial decision buying Tahiti Nui. This was his third night as owner and each one had raucous, all night crowds until closing. Even if the new tsunami lines were draw far inland, he might actually be able to justify pushing the entire building fifteen feet up into the air. The ocean view would be fantastic from that height.

By 2 A.M. John had signed up four new Stand Up Paddling clients based solely on how well he was dancing. They all whispered into his ear that if he could move like that on land, he must be a wizard on the water. He didn't know it yet, but a few tourists in town to buy property determined he was going to be their realtor solely based on his stamina.

By 4 A.M. Captain Tim had retired to his expansive plantation style rental just outside of town. His entourage filled every couch, punee and bed. He sent a text message to the nice lady down the road who would cook breakfast for $8 a head. "Bring extra eggs," the text had said - never ever a problem on this island.

By 5 A.M. the crowd had dwindled to only the hard core dozen or so people that usually closed the place down. Dave had kissed his expansively beautiful date goodnight with a new appreciation for strong women. She had picked him up and spun him around so many times he had lost count. Trish was half asleep in a chair, Kainalu had long since snuck away with Kimo, and Onolani was holding her head up with both hands at a table by the window, next to her sister.

At last call, long after the house band had retired, hours after most tourists had fled to their air conditioned condos and just as the first hints of light glistened in the eastern sky, Pat called in a tab.

"OK, dude. Your drinks tonight are free if you get up on stage and do your thing."

Birdman quietly nodded, reached around behind the bar, retrieved his ancient electric guitar and walked a little stiffly up to the stage. He was wearing another of his signature Dick Brewer surf trunks. The taro fields were still dark but through the windows he could see the light just starting to tickle the mountain peaks beyond. It was time.

Plugging in to the house amp, neglecting the headphones he had used religiously for years and leaving his shirt on, but completely unbuttoned, he bowed to the remaining patrons.

"Good morning," he said softly.

He looked down at his guitar and slowly, easily took everyone remaining on their own private journey to nirvana. Some at the bar swore it was Jimi again, without the twang. Others said it sounded like the Pearl Jam classic *Yellow Ledbetter*. Onolani watched her old lover like she had just met him all over again. When they had explored Hanalei so many years ago he had never played guitar. Now, she thought, it was as if he had descended from rock-n-roll heaven just so everyone would know that it really did exist.

The lone tourist couple still at the bar were enthralled. They were celebrating his recent Nobel Prize for Literature with a trip to Hanalei. His wife noticed tears in his eyes as he watched Birdman carve out the magic with his fingers.

"What's wrong, darling?"

He took her hand and smiled, whispering. "I became a writer because I never could become a guitar player."

ten

~~~

Trish was sprawled out in one of the bedrooms of Hale Ha Ha O'Hanalei, having had to move only a few inches to escape the sun sliding in through her window. Everyone who had closed Tahiti Nui with her were still in their beds. It was 11 A.M.

Poi had managed to signal to the neighbors' cat to come over and push open the door so he could go out. Fortunately, he and the cat had an arrangement. In return for such favors, Poi brought back the fish or lobster remains he occasionally found on his beach walks.

This morning as he wagged his butt in gratitude, he watched the cat walk back to her place, tail held high and a little swagger in her hips. Yes, he daydreamed, if things had turned out a little differently at birth they could have been an item.

As it was, though, things were just fine. Poi, blessed with many things, but not all, knew all too well the secret to happiness. It was being able to see the world from all its fascinating angles, and realizing his scene was one of those angles. His was just as awesome as all the others, only different.

He watched her vanish quietly under her house, no doubt anticipating his next request. He could feel her attraction toward him, just by watching her closely. Cats gave away their every thought with body language. Poi smiled, knowing he would soon reward her interest. With any luck, his next beach walk would produce a dead crab, perfectly toasted by the sun.

The little dog moved easily from those thoughts to others focused on enjoying the late morning. He walked over toward the fence, separating his home from the big yard next door. There, he could watch the little kids frolic at the Aloha School and Daycare Ohana. Their brightly colored clothes, draped over such energetic bodies, moving and jumping, twisting and squealing with so much excitement, captivated him. Finding a sunny spot between the shadows of the ti leaves plants, Poi stretched out in the warm red dirt.

The colors invaded his consciousness as he settled. Butterflies circled his head, brightly colored green geckos chirped nearby, flashing between the contrasting light. Onolani's blue colored-glass garden sparkled in the slowly shifting beams of sun. Poi rested his head on his front paws and looked for a moment beyond and above the rainbow colored children. There the majestically patient mountain peaks played with youthful, frisky clouds, showing them how to grow from wisps into something more substantial. The deep blues just beyond held them all securely, Poi could see, in a big, loving hug.

~~~

Trish, finally up and in front of the bathroom mirror, noticed her skin was bronzing. It would never approach her sister's tone, but it had lost all the pale tattoo of a Chicago winter. Her hair was getting curly with all the humidity and salt from the tropical air. Summers back home had done the same but never with such favor.

Washing her face she loved how the cold water wasn't really so cold that you had to add hot water. It was refreshingly cool. Her eyes, too, were clearer. As late as they had stayed out last night, she had found it unnecessary to drink as heavy as she usually did. Perhaps it had been all the excitement built into the evening. This morning was the first she could remember in a long, long time, where the morning light didn't greet a hangover like an old friend.

Back in the kitchen, Onolani's stash of local Kauai coffee was dwindling fast. Trish would have to remember to buy some more today, perhaps from a road-side stand. She carried a steaming cup of dark beauty with her as she walked down the hallway to see if her sister was home.

Before she made her way to the closed door at the end she saw the old electric guitar, sitting in the hall chair.

"No way..." she whispered to herself, grinning so broadly she had to stop sipping her coffee. Sneaking closer now, to see if it had the famous Jimi Hendrix signature on it, Trish heard a soft voice singing.

It was her sister's voice, sounding sweeter than ever. There was no hoarseness, no east coast accent. There was a lightness to it, a youthfulness that reminded her of when they were kids.

Trish couldn't help but listen a moment longer. She finally heard a man's gentle laughter and then her sister singing the words to "I put a spell on you..." Trish guessed it must be Onolani and Birdman. The signature on the guitar was unmistakable. So too was the joy on the other side of that door.

~~~

Poi was leading the way along the beach, as Trish followed along. He had bounded from behind the ti leaves as she had descended the stairs and grabbed a towel. Now, he thought, he might be able to secure that toasted crab.

The surf had come up significantly during the night, noisily pounding the silence with echoes that reached the far mountain walls. Both of them had to watch for rogue surges that seemed intent on soaking them, rolling them inland a few feet and then sucking them back out, all with terrifying speed.

Poi was especially cognizant of the danger. Short legs might look sexy to cats, but they made swimming an ugly affair. Glancing back at Trish he knew she would be little help in rescuing him. She appeared to be in some kind of trance.

She was indeed. The hehunakai, or surf-generated ocean mist, was billowing above her, moving slowly toward the parking lot and beach homes. In that mist, scraps of rainbow teased the sunlight on and off as they took turns angling properly toward Trish's gaze. The scent of the sea, subtle and without any brine, invited her to breathe as deeply as possible. Her chest expanded with the efforts to bring as much of it inside her as possible. It tasted anciently familiar.

The rough sand no longer irritated her bare feet, but awarded her tenacious efforts to toughen them with a gentle massage. It might have been her imagination, something she was now acknowledging might be in hyper-drive, but her legs were feeling stronger.

After another few minutes, Trish scooped up Poi and held him safely in her arms. The ocean was full of energy like a teenager at an unchaperoned dance. The water twisted and turned and shouted out to all who might join it. In fact, Trish noticed, there were people out in the water on boogie boards.

She stood a little higher up on the beach and watched. Young kids, maybe high school age, literally fell down the faces of the larger shore-breaking waves, disappeared under an unimaginable explosion of whitewater and moments later bounced back up, riding the rest of the wave right up to the sand. They looked terrified. But only until they knew they had made it in safely, at which point they promptly turned back out to sea and swam as fast as they could to catch another.

Abandoning the shoreline, Trish and Poi both walked a couple of blocks inland, along the edge of the taro fields. The deep green of the triangular leaves, reaching strongly up from their pools of clear mountain water, were grabbing as much of the sun's energy as they could. Trish thought she could see them actually shaking in their effort to suck in as much of the light as possible.

Poi was swimming in the warm waters pushing the stems to the side as he navigated alongside Trish, her bare feet now embedded in the mud beneath it all. Her toes relished in the secret coolness there that no one else could feel.

Trish knew at that moment she was in trouble.

She was in a gang fight and her crew numbered only one. The other crew included the surfer girls who coyly smiled as they ran past her on the beach, holding impossibly small boards under athletic arms. And the handsome kayak instructors who thanked their stars for the low paying job they enjoyed going to every day. The taro farmers, the fresh air, the clean ocean, the warm sunshine, the lack of a desire to drink alcohol. They were all conspiring against her in an attempt to have her forget everything that came before.

   She wasn't sure if this was a bad thing or not, something like marijuana. It felt good, but she knew it wasn't the normal way to feel things - it was artificial, induced, solicited. Internal warning bells rang louder. A warning that, despite any evidence, screamed there was a weapon of mass destruction that would most certainly destroy her way of life forever - if she stayed.

eleven

~~~

Twenty-five hundred and sixty-one point one four miles away, some twelve point five miles below the frigid waters of Queen Charlotte Island, Canada, the big iron bell was preparing to ring. It had already rung some six times this month, all around the Pacific Rim. The fractured rocky coastline nearby could feel the tiny vibrations that heralded such ringing. However, those that listened out for such sounds sat quietly in their over air-conditioned government offices and drank coffee, waiting. Their own machines measured the tiny songs as well, but were stuck inside an amazingly primitive technology. Prediction was still a dark art. It was the rocky coastline though, experienced beyond anything the caffeine fans could imagine, that knew this time was different.

~~~

Trish and Poi couldn't feel it, either. They climbed out of the taro fields and walked the thin path beside the road back toward Hanalei. The red dirt felt warm, almost inviting and she laughed as she now understood Poi's predilection to roll around in it.

It was early afternoon and the middle aged haole ladies were flitting around outside their dress and jewelry shops. Some of them changed what was hanging outside; others simply looked around, smiled at their good fortune and went back to their customers.

They had moved here when they were very young women, never having found a need or desire to leave, ever. These jobs allowed them to swim in the bay at morning or play in a waterfall before dark. Working in a surf or dress shop helped them make ends meet only because for them those ends were not far away from each other. Simple living was the key to enjoying time.

Making their way down farther, Trish saw dozens of clean rental cars pulling into the Ching Young Village shops. There those shoppers might secure proof they were in Hanalei with a self-designated t-shirt. Here at least the designs were captivating, created by those enthralled with living here.

Poi ran up to each of the whale-watching boat kiosks, as if cute was a currency they might accept. It wasn't. The local kids working these places were anxious to complete their shift. Then off they would run, to surf, to hike the mountains, perhaps to play with their nieces and nephews at the river or way up in the jungles where no tourist had ever been.

The only people who looked like their day was actually busy were the cooks at the L & L BBQ. There was something about ginger and teriyaki that made you work and move quickly.

After taking her time to enjoy a peanut butter, banana and strawberry smoothie Trish started making her way back to Hale Ha Ha O'Hanalei. The afternoon was slowly slipping away. Her sister would probably be up and about now, dancing around the kitchen ready to tell her all about how the Earth had moved.

~~~

Indeed it was about to, needed to - actually had a most incredible urge to do so. Immeasurable forces were propelling hundreds of miles of the Earth's crust to slip under the North American plate. It had been a battle waging for some three years and now the Pacific plate was going to win, forcing its way another significant step lower.

The sky was dark above the nervously frigid waters. They could feel the subtle vibrations in the crust below. With all of their salty weight, they continued pushing downward with a suppressing force, hoping that the massive warriors beneath them would delay their battle.

The sun was still well above the horizon in Hanalei, above Ke'e beach, above the Kalalau trail and the Na Pali coastline. Sequestered in their isolation and warmth the Hawaiian Islands basked peacefully, unaware of any trouble from afar.

The sea around Queen Charlotte Island moved uneasily, feeling more vibrations of the fight below her initiate. If only, the waters felt, they could press more firmly against the massive plates then they might be spared their neighbors' sudden violent spasms. The massive waters tried vainly to summon the great weight of the atmosphere as well. Together they might suppress the volatile rock beneath the both of them.

Yet, despite some small successes in the recent past, this was a futile effort. As Trish and Poi took their afternoon naps, as Kainalu swam under a large wave at the bay, as everyone else in Hanalei enjoyed the last of a spectacular day, the big iron bell rang.

5:04 P.M. went unnoticed by everyone on the island of Kauai. Queen Charlotte Island's calm, though, was shattered by the violence from far beneath her. As the massive energy pulse moved up from twelve miles below, slamming into the disappointed sea, a displacement caused the sea to pulse up and out. The waters spasmed in all directions as well as slapping the massive atmosphere atop it, showering those close by with spray. Seals on the still warm rocks felt as if an Orca had found them; seagulls encountered the spray, stalled and fell through the turbulent air just above the waters. The caffeine fans in their offices noted the magnitude, with some excitement. Mother Earth was throwing dice again and this time her number appeared lucky indeed: 7 point 7.

~~~

Cecil was half way to Lihue, fuming in the back of his chauffeured limo. He had planned to fire the driver again this morning, but realized he was rapidly running out of homeless, down-on-their-luck men that he hadn't already fired. Kauai was, he noted with some disgust, too small of an island. He would have to fly one over from Maui, as soon as he took care of this land swindle with the Kauai Land Board.

His 6 P.M. appointment was rare, but the chairman had agreed after Cecil had insisted, declaring his intention to cancel all the checks he had written to various Hanalei organizations.

"Hey, boss," the overly helpful driver announced over the speaker. "Big earthquake just now on the West Coast."

Cecil interrupted practicing the rant he intended to deliver and simply stared at his driver. Why was this hobo even talking to him? He didn't want to be his friend; he didn't want any kind of a conversation. He did want an employee that would simply respond like a mouse-click on a computer. Do as my finger says. He ignored the driver.

They drove for another mile, passing through the slow moving traffic of Kapa'a. The bars and restaurants, even the Hotel Coral Reef were all putting on their neon lights for the evening. People jaywalked as best they could, dodging those intent on getting home twenty seconds earlier than they might have going the speed limit.

"Hey, boss," the driver tried again.

Cecil dropped his head in desperation. He never had this problem back in New York. There, the drivers kept their mouths shut, and drove! Here, everyone wanted to chat! It was infuriating!

"What the hell...?" Cecil barked.

The driver, ignoring or missing the anger in his employer's voice, started talking over him. "Radio says a tidal wave is coming."

"What?"

"Yeah, you know, a tidal wave... what do they call it? Tsunami, I think..."

Cecil sat forward. "Turn up the radio!"

The driver nodded to himself, happy in the fact that he had actually been helpful. A tip might magically appear this evening, giving him a chance to enjoy a cold *forty* tonight.

The radio crackled on the speakers next to Cecil. He leaned back and closed his eyes. Immediately he was there, again. The courtroom in the Bronx. His parents on either side of him, standing, an inexpensive lawyer next to his father. He had taken a long deep breath then, awaiting the judge's verdict.

Thirty days of community service. As devastating as that had been to him and his family back as a teenager, he would take it all over again tonight. Anything but a tsunami!

"... the first wave is expected to impact the north shore of Kauai at 10:28 P.M. Oahu at 10:43..."

Cecil gripped the seat, feeling his fingers ache with the futile effort to strangle the world, strangle it for conspiring against him.

"Turn around," he whispered, out of breath.

The driver was stopped at a crosswalk, watching colorful beach towels move around young female hips in that unique way they are apt to do. He hadn't heard anything from the back of the car. His ears were consumed with the nearly forgotten echoes of chasing such girls.

Cecil leaned forward and banged hard on the glass. "Turn around!"

~~~

Dave was already packing his bags. An evacuation order had not yet been issued. He had received the text alert on his phone about a minute after the event. The Queen Charlotte Islands, despite being so prone to larger quakes, had no buoys installed offshore. No buoys that would give scientists a semi-accurate indication of how large a tsunami pulse was.

He had already reviewed the calculations for arrival time. There was no doubt a tsunami would indeed arrive. Every coastal earthquake generated one; it was just that most of them were tiny. The great oceans were constantly being crisscrossed with pulses of energy. Small submerged landslides, iceberg calving, even the very vibrations of ship engines were all measurable. The vast majority were simply data points of no consequence. But you needed deep ocean buoys and tide gauges along various coastlines to give you any semblance of predictive certainty of about the size of a wave.

Dave knew where the buoys were, and where the buoys had been before Washington budget cuts had doomed the very ones they needed tonight. Therefore, his friends at the Pacific Tsunami Warning Center, on O'ahu, would be giving it their best educated guess.

He threw his last pair of socks in his bag, zipped it shut and headed for his rental car. If he hurried he would beat the traffic and chaos of an evacuation, maybe even secure a room at the Princeville Resort, high enough above sea level to be safe. That evacuation order was still to come, but he understood that if scientists had to guess, they would always err on the conservative side. That meant a certain evacuation of every coastline in the State of Hawaii.

~~~

Trish opened the door for Poi, letting him run in first. If Onolani and Birdman were still there, then Poi rushing at their feet, butt wagging and tongue flapping would alert them to her arrival. Catching her sister naked, or worse yet, her and Birdman naked, was not something she wanted to happen.

She listened for her sister's voice greeting her little dog, but heard nothing. Perhaps they were down at the beach, or still sequestered in their love nest. That term, nest, came to her mind, despite how strange it sounded, and for good reason.

Hanalei was like a nest, a spirit nest. Trish sat down on the punee and rested, looking up into the papaya trees just outside the screen walls. Some birds flew away from this nest into the big world, some visited and returned home. And, some birds never left - for better or worse, she couldn't quite tell. Trapped was a word that was slowly trying to work its way into her internal discussion.

Disney World had held the same magical power over her, as a child. She had cried and cried when her parents declared it time to leave. It had taken them four hours to find her that night after she broke their grip and ran. By the time they had, dozens of worried employees trailing behind them, a sobbing and terrified Trish had already felt the magic leave her. She had hidden in places that were never meant to be visited: dark crawlspaces where the old turkey legs fell, behind smelly garbage bins yet to be emptied, places where sticky half-eaten lollipops had stuck to her shorts in the dark.

Hanalei would certainly leave her as well, she knew. Something would eventually appear to destroy the feeling. The magic was only a ruse. It would break her heart as well. Being single her entire life had taught her well - risk nothing, cry never.

~~~

Birdman walked down the hallway, Poi trying desperately to lick his feet to taste what he might have been up to in his master's room. The tanned, athletically muscled gray haired man wrapped a beach towel around his waist right before he entered the TV room.

Trish turned to see him finish tucking one end under the other, securing from view all curiosities.

"Good afternoon, Sister Trish," he said, turning toward her. He reached up and ran both hands through his long hair, flexing his bare chest. "Or, should I say, good evening, already?"

Unconsciously, Trish tried to sit up, unaware that her blush was giving her away. After a moment she stood up, grinning.

"I'm not really a Sister, you know. A nun..."

Birdman laughed, grinning right back at Trish. She thought her eyes drifted for a moment to where the towel was tied, but she couldn't be sure.

"I know, sorry." He walked up to her, his hand out. "A pleasure to meet you, Trish."

Trish saw it all in slow motion. His six pack stomach flexing as he walked, his strong thighs pushing the colorful towel forward as he confidently approached her. His spectacular smile was piercing any propriety she might still have left.

"They call me..."

"Yes, yes," Trish said quickly. "Birdman." She went to shake his hand.

"Nah, give me a hug, sister!"

Trish sighed deeply. She knew the drill. She had dreamed it a thousand times. Tall, handsome, muscular, half-naked man hugged her. Her welcoming arms went around him, feeling with only her fingertips his firm strong flesh there, pulling him in closer. His massive, hairy chest pushed into her quivering breasts, enveloping her entire being with masculinity, power and an overwhelming desire to lick his neck...

Birdman felt the woman shivering in his arms, and politely pulled back, holding her at arm's length.

"Did you just lick my neck?"

Horrified, Trish pulled away, swept her face into her hands and turned.

"Sorry, sorry! It's... it's just a habit I'm afraid."

He laughed again, that same heart-shattering expression of happiness every romance novel, every dream, every love story she had ever heard about always had. His voice lowered as he confirmed, "Well, let me tell you, it felt good!"

Trish turned to find Birdman walking away from her, to the kitchen for coffee. Her eyes focused on the back of his towel as it disappeared behind the kitchen counter.

"But," Birdman said, catching her focus as it quickly moved up to his eyes. "Another time, another place, you know. Another life." He poured the black liquid into a turtle-decorated ceramic mug. "Onolani is my soul mate this time around."

"Of course, I'm so, so sorry to have done..."

"Trish," Birdman said. "I can't blame you, honey girl. You are a beautiful, sexy woman, there's no doubt. And, I'm a gift from the gods!" He laughed again, this time so hard his towel fell off his hips.

Trish unconsciously stood a little higher on her toes, but it was no help. Birdman bent down, picked up his towel, and wrapped it around his narrow hips. He might have been moving in slow motion on purpose, but it might have been her mind racing.

"Excuse my nakedness, young lady, but I have yet to find my clothes!" He said this in some kind of Shakespearean accent, with a flourish of his hand into the air.

Embarrassed, she fled to the outside lanai overlooking the bay. Alone there, she closed her eyes, only to begin to feel it again. That inexorable pull at her heart, this time from within. It had been a long, long time since she had been loved. It was yet another promise Hanalei was making to her. Similar to the one that said it would always caress her in a warm sea, or dazzle her imagination with its jungled mountains. It also promised to sparkle her laughter with a giddy appreciation of never being cold again. It all added up to a whisper in her quite receptive mind - saying that her life could be vibrant and wonderful here, beyond imagination.

Trish wrapped her arms around herself, tightly, feeling her body tremble. She was slowly being drugged, this she knew. Intoxicated, not by the wisps of pakalolo in the air, but by something far more compelling, the touch of angels. The angels of paradise summoning her abstinence-ridden soul back to a party she had left a long time ago.

A tear of frustration rolled slowly down her cheek. Just as it touched her lips, the first of the civil defense sirens shrieked throughout the valley.

~~~

Pat turned on the TV in his office at Tahiti Nui when the first siren went off. Impatient for the details he knew he wouldn't get from local news, he found the website for the Pacific Tsunami Warning Center. It had been bookmarked on his laptop as he had researched the deal to buy the bar. He stared for a moment out the window, thinking he might actually see the *god of irony* laughing at him from afar.

Tipping up what would be the first of many Mai Tais he read the stark announcement:

BULLETIN

```
TSUNAMI MESSAGE NUMBER    3
NWS PACIFIC TSUNAMI WARNING CENTER EWA BEACH HI
709 PM HST SAT OCT 27 2012

TO - CIVIL DEFENSE IN THE STATE OF HAWAII

SUBJECT - TSUNAMI WARNING

A TSUNAMI WARNING IS ISSUED FOR THE STATE OF HAWAII
EFFECTIVE AT 0709 PM HST.  THIS UPGRADE IS DUE TO THE
SEA LEVEL READINGS RECEIVED AND THE RESULTING CHANGE IN
THE HAWAII TSUNAMI FORECAST.

AN EARTHQUAKE HAS OCCURRED WITH THESE PRELIMINARY
PARAMETERS

     ORIGIN TIME - 0504 PM HST 27 OCT 2012
     COORDINATES - 52.8 NORTH   131.8 WEST
     LOCATION    - QUEEN CHARLOTTE ISLANDS REGION
     MAGNITUDE   - 7.7  MOMENT

MEASUREMENTS OR REPORTS OF TSUNAMI WAVE ACTIVITY

 GAUGE LOCATION          LAT   LON    TIME       AMPL
PER
 -------------------     ----- ------  -----
 ---------------    -----
 DART 46404              45.9N 128.8W  0417Z   0.05M /
 0.2FT  20MIN
 LANGARA POINT BC        54.2N 133.1W  0424Z   0.20M /
 0.7FT  26MIN
 DART 46419              48.8N 129.6W  0346Z   0.06M /
 0.2FT  12MIN

 LAT  - LATITUDE (N-NORTH, S-SOUTH)
```

LON - LONGITUDE (E-EAST, W-WEST)
 TIME - TIME OF THE MEASUREMENT (Z IS UTC IS GREENWICH
TIME)
 AMPL - TSUNAMI AMPLITUDE MEASURED RELATIVE TO NORMAL
SEA LEVEL.
          IT IS ...NOT... CREST-TO-TROUGH WAVE HEIGHT.
          VALUES ARE GIVEN IN BOTH METERS(M) AND FEET(FT).
 PER - PERIOD OF TIME IN MINUTES(MIN) FROM ONE WAVE TO
THE NEXT.

 NOTE - DART MEASUREMENTS ARE FROM THE DEEP OCEAN AND
THEY ARE GENERALLY MUCH SMALLER THAN WOULD BE COASTAL
MEASUREMENTS AT SIMILAR LOCATIONS.

EVALUATION

 A TSUNAMI HAS BEEN GENERATED THAT COULD CAUSE DAMAGE
ALONG COASTLINES OF ALL ISLANDS IN THE STATE OF HAWAII.
URGENT ACTION SHOULD BE TAKEN TO PROTECT LIVES AND
PROPERTY.

 A TSUNAMI IS A SERIES OF LONG OCEAN WAVES. EACH
INDIVIDUAL WAVE CREST CAN LAST 5 TO 15 MINUTES OR MORE
AND EXTENSIVELY FLOOD COASTAL AREAS. THE DANGER CAN
CONTINUE FOR MANY HOURS AFTER THE INITIAL WAVE AS
SUBSEQUENT WAVES ARRIVE. TSUNAMI WAVE HEIGHTS CANNOT BE
PREDICTED AND THE FIRST WAVE MAY NOT BE THE LARGEST.

TSUNAMI WAVES EFFICIENTLY WRAP AROUND ISLANDS. ALL
SHORES ARE AT RISK NO MATTER WHICH DIRECTION THEY FACE.
THE TROUGH OF A TSUNAMI WAVE MAY TEMPORARILY EXPOSE THE
SEAFLOOR BUT THE AREA WILL QUICKLY FLOOD AGAIN.

EXTREMELY STRONG AND UNUSUAL NEARSHORE CURRENTS CAN
ACCOMPANY A TSUNAMI. DEBRIS PICKED UP AND CARRIED BY A
TSUNAMI AMPLIFIES ITS DESTRUCTIVE POWER. SIMULTANEOUS
HIGH TIDES OR HIGH SURF CAN SIGNIFICANTLY INCREASE THE
TSUNAMI HAZARD.

THE ESTIMATED ARRIVAL TIME IN HAWAII OF THE FIRST
TSUNAMI WAVE IS

                  1028 PM HST SAT 27 OCT 2012

MESSAGES WILL BE ISSUED HOURLY OR SOONER AS CONDITIONS
WARRANT.

Pat quickly walked back out to the bar. All five employees were nervously cleaning up and turned to look at him. The four remaining patrons were quickly downing their drinks and walking out.

Pat put his arms up in the air. "See you tomorrow, kids. Good luck!"

They all dropped what they were doing and gathered their belongings.

"Wait," Pat said, going back behind the bar. He began setting bottles of liquor up on the counter. "Everyone take a bottle, it might be a long night."

~~~

The cold, briny waters off Queen Charlotte Island had taken quite a hit from below. They had been pushed violently upward as the Pacific plate insisted and now there was nothing the ocean could do about it. That energy pulse had quickly departed in all directions of the compass, quickly swamping the rocky cliffs full of seals and birds and racing toward the inner reaches of the sounds and remote coastlines in western Canada. However, the majority of the energy had been focused in a twenty-eight degree arch toward the southwest open ocean. Toward the equator, toward Hawaii.

In the cold darkness, it raced through the deep waters, sneaking beneath the Matson cargo ships headed to Seattle, unnoticed. Amazing that such a destructive force could hide so well, especially one that was traveling at 681.7 kilometers per hour. It would also slip silently below and pass the Hawaiian Airlines flight from New York to Honolulu, already a hundred miles out over the Pacific.

~~~

Cecil's driver was driving as fast as he thought he could without crashing. It wasn't fast enough.

"Come on!" Cecil complained. "Can you imagine the traffic? I need my bags, and then we have to get the hell out of Hanalei before the chaos."

"Yes, sir."

As they passed the Princeville resort fountain, the driver had to start braking. The rapidly approach ninety degree turn to the left convinced all but the insane that it was to be respected. The rears tires spun once, then grabbed the pavement again, holding until the small limo straightened out.

Cecil looked to his right as they descended into Hanalei valley, spying dozens of cars already heading out. This was the beginning of the panic, he figured.

"Step on it; people are bailing out already!"

The driver didn't speak, electing to spend every scrap of his mental energy on controlling the car down the steep cliff face road. Just as he thought he had the car under his control, he saw a pile of red lights just around the corner ahead.

Cecil felt the deceleration and looked ahead just in time to see why he was falling forward against the glass.

The driver felt the car moving slightly off to the right, and the cliff. With both feet on the brakes and each arm fighting the steering wheel, they stopped. Inches. Away.

"Goddammit," Cecil complained. "Ease up a bit!"

They sat there for a full minute as four or five cars moved past them, headed out of the valley. Finally, they pulled forward, following the six cars ahead of them.

"Damn bridge ahead," Cecil said out loud. "I hate that bridge!"

A county sign just in front of the bridge said "Local Courtesy 4 - 5 cars at a time"

The first of the cars ahead of Cecil crested the bridge just as the second car entered. Several large pickup trucks were waiting their turn. They had favorite chairs, aunties and uncles all piled high in the back of their beds. The drivers all looked intently at each of the cars going into Hanalei, broadcasting their impatience with nervous stares.

Cecil's driver watched the fifth car, in the group of seven he was in, cross the bridge. He expected the sixth, just in front of him to stop. But, it didn't.

"Follow him, don't stop!" Cecil barked. "Go! Go! Go!"

The driver pushed down on the gas just as he saw the expected movement of the big truck across the bridge.

The nervous and impatient pickup truck guy was counting cars. He only had to wait for four, maybe five. But as he saw number six begin to cross, he let his foot off the brake roughly, lurching ahead slightly.

Cecil and his driver had fallen a bit behind number six. The big pickup truck couldn't wait anymore and entered the bridge.

"Back up!" the pickup driver yelled.

"What the ..." Cecil swore.

The pickup driver had a crying baby in the back, a drunk uncle in a chair in the flat bed, and his pregnant wife swearing how she hated this bridge. The last thing he was going to put up with was a fancy car trying to muscle its way across the bridge.

He got on his horn, never slowing down.

Cecil couldn't believe his eyes. "He's going to run into us!"

His driver had stopped and was frantically trying to put the short limo into reverse, but he was a little too slow.

The big pickup truck's railroad tie bumper swept easily up the Mercedes' bumper, peeling paint and a fine layer of aluminum up ahead of it.

"Back up!" the pickup truck driver screamed. "Back up!" His diesel locomotive horn was striking terror into Cecil's driver, who was having flashbacks about that train crossing gate he had run as a teenager.

Cecil ducked. His own driver fell to the side just as the bumper came to rest against the windshield, cracking it. In a moment the big truck settled slowly and inexorably into the engine compartment of the Mercedes.

~~~

"How long do we have," Trish asked. "Before it hits?"

Birdman was setting an alarm on his watch. "One hour forty three."

"A little less than two hours," Onolani said, interpreting with a laugh.

"Hey, if we're going down to the beach, I want to know exactly how long before I gotta bail," Birdman dismissed the criticism. "Are you coming, Trish?"

Trish had heard him say "...going down to the beach" but thought she must have misheard. Wasn't that a bad idea when a tsunami was coming? She turned to Onolani, hoping to get an explanation.

"Trish, honey." Onolani smiled, patiently looking at her with hands pressed together in front of her purple and yellow tye-dye muu-muu. "We intend to chant the tsunami into nothing," she waved her hands apart now, as if shooing flies. "It will simply kiss our toes and disappear into the bad idea it always was."

Birdman was shaking his head no. "Ono, I'm out of there at 10:15 P.M., tops!"

Onolani took a deep breath, trying to expel the dagger just implanted into her confidence. He wasn't being helpful, despite promising he would play his guitar for the chanters. When facing a force of nature, in the dark and barefoot, she needed conviction. Not an escape schedule.

"Wait, wait, wait," Trish interrupted, shaking the silly idea from her head. The idea fell down onto her tongue, and out. "You're going to the beach to stop a tsunami, with chanting?"

Birdman nodded silently and smiled, pointing to his watch.

Onolani put her hands on her hips, tilted her head slightly and complained. "When you say it like that, sure! It sounds crazy." She tilted her head to the other side and dropped her hands to better talk. "Hanalei needs us to try to be our most powerful tonight. We shall collectively voice our prayers to Gaia, asking that the great waves lay down softly onto the sand."

Trish felt her mouth close, after hanging open in surprise. She glanced up quickly to Birdman, who again pointed at his watch. He then nodded toward her sister.

"Who is going with you two?" Trish looked quickly down to Poi.

"Only a half a dozen of the..." Onolani paused. "Six of us." She glanced down at her precious little dog and then looked to her sister. "Will you please take Poi to Princeville, though? Just in case."

~~~

Honolulu-style road rage was unknown on Kauai for the most part, and this rare example drew everyone out of their now parked vehicles. The pickup truck driver's crew spilled out of the cab and the flat bed. The three or four pickup trucks that were following him, and were partially up on the bridge as well, came out to gawk as well.

Cecil, climbed out, incredulous. He could feel the veins in his neck throbbing; swollen and pumping venom furiously. He half-wished he had the fangs to deliver it. Walking right past his still terrified driver, laying on the front seat, and up to the pickup truck driver, Cecil glared at the man.

"You're going to pay big for this!"

The pickup truck driver spat to the side. "You can collect at your funeral..." he paused. "Hey, I know who you are! You're that developer from Maui, who wants to build another Princeville!" He stepped a bit closer, waving his people closer.

Both men held back for as long as they could. Traffic backed up in both directions. Most times such a crash afforded everyone an opportunity to sit back and enjoy the view, waiting for tow trucks. This time it was different. It was dark, and people were either escaping Hanalei or driving home to pick someone up who needed to escape. The tension from those stuck behind Cecil flowed into his arms, shaking with anger. The anger from those behind the pickup truck driver, infuriated that the Mercedes had insisted on breaking bridge etiquette, fumed forth as well.

Right before Cecil intended to bite the pickup truck driver's neck to inject the deadly venom, his own driver spilled out of the front seat of the Mercedes, along with an half empty vodka bottle. The bottle shattered the silence of the stand off, delightfully letting the glass rattle musically along the steel frame of the bridge.

"Oh, brah!" the pickup driver yelled, pointing at the bottle. "You guys are frickin' bobo!" He turned to his supportive crowd and announced. "Hey, the guy who wants to turn our taro fields into another Princeville...this is him!"

Boos and jeers began erupting, as well as several irritated car horns. More of the men walked forward.

"And, check it out," the pickup truck driver continued as Cecil's driver scrambled twice, tripped and finally retrieved his vodka bottle. "They're drinking and driving, too!"

Immediately, Cecil realized his hopes of revenge were doomed. This big local guy would never have to pay for the damage now. He marched over to the side of the bridge, pushing his driver hard in the chest.

"You're fired!"

More boos and jeers erupted and now car horns from behind Cecil began blaring.

Cecil's driver, although not drunk, intended to now become so, and quickly walked back up toward Princeville. He slid the vodka bottle securely up into his silly black driver's coat.

The pickup truck driver turned, waved everyone back and yelled out, "We gotta clear the bridge, give us some room!"

Several cars behind the pickup trucks pulled off to the side, giving everyone room enough to reverse and clear the bridge. The lead truck, backed off of the Mercedes, taking the hood and front bumper with it.

"Clear the bridge!"

Cecil began hearing it from all directions, like a chant. Both sides of the bridge were yelling it now. He turned to his retreating driver.

"Hey, come back here and move this car!"

Henry, that man formally known as Cecil's driver, turned and flipped off his ex-boss. He was high enough up on the hill to see the top of the bridge. The bright headlights painting the scene below appeared to him as the gates of hell must to those running out and away.

"Hey!" Cecil yelled again in his direction.

Henry took off his silly driver's hat and with every ounce of freedom he could muster, sailed the hat out and over the entire scene. The boos and jeers quickly turned to cheers as everyone, including Cecil, watched the hat sail over their heads and gently land into the Hanalei River.

~~~

Traffic was backed up from the bridge all the way into Hanalei town now. Pat looked out at the line of cars all pointing toward the exit, turned back into the bar and picked up another bottle to take with him.

Trish and Poi were in Onolani's car unable to turn off of Mahimahi Street onto the main road. Cars were backed up more and more toward Hanalei school. Despite her better judgment, she checked her watch, and figured she had enough time to see what her sister was really up to at the beach.

The first wave was due in an hour.

~~~

Cecil was standing next to his wrecked Mercedes, unsure how he might drive it off the bridge. The chant to "clear the bridge" was quickly becoming a roar, with a symphony of accompanying car horns.

The lead pickup truck driver's cell phone rang. He got word that traffic was now backed up to the school. He turned to gather eight of his buddies from the trucks behind him, and together they marched back up onto the bridge.

Cecil stood his ground as they approached, but reached for his cell phone to dial 911. He scolded himself for not doing so earlier. Now, it appeared, a gang of men were coming to accost him.

Shaking, his fingers couldn't dial. He glanced up to see them standing right in front of him.

"Can you drive this thing or what?" the lead pickup truck driver demanded.

"Hell no, look what you did to the engine!" Cecil fought out the words, hoping they sounded intimidating. They didn't.

"OK, guys; get behind and push."

Seven of the guys moved behind the Mercedes as the lead pickup truck driver reached in the open driver's window and grabbed the steering wheel.

"What are you doing?" Cecil demanded, trying to push the lead pickup truck driver away from his car.

That earned him a firm shove into the chest as well as "We're clearing the bridge!"

It took a few good pushes to free the Mercedes from the bridge, but it soon started to roll. With no one working the brakes, assuming they even worked, the battered vehicle began moving faster toward the clear end of the bridge.

What no one planned on was the fact that the car would continue to roll. It dropped over the edge of the bridge, lower onto the sloping asphalt and continued.

The lead pickup driver had already pulled his arm out of the window and the seven friends behind the Mercedes had quit pushing. The car moved down to the left, off the main road and toward the first of hundreds of taro fields.

Cecil ran after it when he saw its destination. "Stop! Stop my car!"

The local guys had only wanted the damaged Mercedes off the bridge and the road. A few of them took tentative steps toward it, as if they might try and grab the rear bumper. Quickly, they saw the momentum, though, and gave up.

Cecil stopped at the edge of the taro field and watched as his short Mercedes limo plunged headlong into the water. As the rear wheels settled into the water the entire car gave a gasp and sank to the roof.

Traffic immediately began moving, everyone now taking the five car turns, as two women from the lead pickup truck stayed to direct. A moment later, police officers arrived with lights.

The original pickup trucks departed soon thereafter, laughing and shouting at Cecil.

"Hey, that's a good idea! Luxury houses built atop luxury cars!"

~~~

The civil defense sirens were again throwing their alerts out in all directions, just as a Civil Air Patrol Cessna cruised over the bay doing the same thing.

Trish and Poi had found Birdman and Onolani down at the bay. Trish was intent on trying to convince Birdman to insure her sister wouldn't be left in danger.

"Seriously, though, Ono," Trish implored one last time. Her argument made even less sense down on the beach, surrounded by like-minded chanters, than it did back at the house. "You saw the videos of the Japan tsunami, right?"

Onolani took one last moment, interrupted as she was, and hugged her sister. "Keep Poi safe, that's your part. My part is here, making the tsunami go away."

Birdman tapped Trish on the shoulder just then, pointed to his watch and mouthed silently, "don't worry." He went back to playing his guitar, a gentle rendition of something the Beatles might have done, or perhaps the Boston Philharmonic. It was difficult to tell with only a single electric guitar and a small amp.

Trish stood baffled at what she saw as a gross misunderstanding of nature. She scoffed at the others standing around, chanting with her sister. Many were dressed in white linen, others in jeans and hats. No flashlights, no candles. At night. Every one of them was standing in the shallow waters, facing the open sea, clapping hands together mostly, and singing softly. At least, Trish noticed, the huge surf had subsided to a gentle caress.

Turning to walk back to the car, she looked back once more toward the group. There they stood, stoic in the full moon's light, beautiful in their ignorance, beautiful in their determination.

Trish noticed the Civil Air Patrol plane making its way slowly farther west, out toward the Na Pali coast, a bright searchlight shining down from above. She hugged Poi and started the car.

There was only so much a person could do.

~~~

Pat had his SUV packed and slowly pulled out into the thinning traffic. Most everyone that intended to seek safety on high ground had done so already. The cook had stayed on with Pat to help pack as much of the valuable items as possible: the signed photos of famous Hollywood types that had visited, the computer files and the ones that hadn't been converted yet, and most importantly the "secret stash" of specialty booze. Pat didn't know that this cache had even existed. The cook had finally explained that it had always been a tradition, since his own grandfather had flipped omelets here, that when certain members of the former Hawaiian royalty came to visit, the "stash" was brought out.

With that secured, Pat pulled out slowly onto the main road. Immediately, the cook spotted hitchhikers ahead.

"Well," Pat said. "I don't normally pick up hitchhikers, but when I do, it's during a tsunami evacuation."

~~~

The '68 BMW sedan had sputtered to a stop after only four minutes of driving. John had been determined to save it, if anything. It was his prize automobile, but one that had not been driven in at least a year. The three stand-up paddle boards on the roof were almost as important, and then there was Taylor, his latest squeeze, a distant but necessary third.

"What's wrong with this old heap?" she demanded.

"Hey," John said. "This is a classic; I can't leave it for the wave to take." He turned the key again, but the engine ignored the request to start. That's when the steam began curling out from under the hood.

Taylor sighed, opened the passenger side door and swung her legs out. "Are you sure this is what you wear to a tsunami, John?"

He turned and watched her see-thru beach cover do exactly what it was supposed to do: hint at the wonders just beneath.

"Wear something you can swim in," John laughed. "That's the latest fashion trend on the island, trust me." He hid the keys under the seat and opened his own door. "We're going to have to get a ride."

"Oh, goodie!" Taylor exclaimed. "I'm sensational at doing that!"

~~~

Pat saw that the man and woman were leaning against a broken down car, the girl had her thumb out and her leg seductively poised just outside of her pareo.

"I dunno, boss," the cook said. "She looks too good to be for real. Might be a trap, ya know."

Pat slowed and put on his right blinker. Quickly scanning the nearby bushes and hiding places, he felt confident there were no bad guys waiting to car-jack them. "You might be right, but the guy she is with doesn't fit. He's way too clean cut."

As it became clear they were getting a ride, Taylor started jumping up and down and waving her arms. That alone could stop traffic, but Pat was first in line to pick them up.

Taylor came bounding up to the passenger window, pushing her big mop of curls inside.

"Are you going uphill?"

Pat laughed out loud, as the cook sat back and took in the view.

"Of course, but the back is full," Pat said, looking into the small back seat. "You two will have to ride up in here."

John climbed into the rear seat while the cook slid over to the middle of the front seat.

"No, please," Taylor insisted. "I have to sit in the middle, always."

The cook slid back over, climbed out of the truck and watched the dressed-for-a-tsunami fashion statement bound into the cab.

"Why the middle?" Pat asked, his curiosity beaming at his good fortune, evident now, in picking up hitchhikers.

"Oh, honey," Taylor exclaimed as if the entire world already understood it. "In a pickup truck, the girl always sits right next to the driver."

~~~

Cecil stood just off the bridge and stared at his car in the taro field. He hadn't even started construction and already things were not going his way. He looked up at the moonlit jungle mountain cliffs and nodded some small acquiescence. Maybe it hadn't been the best idea.

Cars and trucks and jeeps all took their turns crossing the bridge, but it soon appeared no one was entering Hanalei valley any longer. Without a way to get back to his rental, he reluctantly figured it was time to walk uphill.

He crossed the bridge as rental cars sped across, ignoring him. As he rounded the curve that began the steep incline up the cliff and out to Princeville, an old but brightly painted Volkswagen bus stopped. The side door slid open, revealing soft lighting and the faint wisps of incense.

"Hop in, dude," a man's voice said from the shadows.

Cecil waved politely and continued walking. He had no intention of interacting with any more people tonight, least of all hippies in a VW van. The van waited.

The few cars behind them saw the walker and patiently gave the VW a chance to pick the guy up.

"Cecil?" a woman's voice asked.

Cecil stopped and turned. It was too dark to make out any faces.

"Cecil, Cecil, Cecil! I can't believe it's you, babe!"

Cecil tried to look inside the van but the light was just too dim.

"Who is this?"

"Oh, Cecil. It's Kainalu, remember? From back in the Makena beach days?"

"Hop in, dude," the original man's voice said again.

"Come on, Cecil," Kainalu said. "We're only going up to the Princeville fountain. Big party, honey. Like the old days, you know."

Cecil stood there transfixed for a moment. In his life experience of late, when things were going badly, they usually continued to move in that direction. For a long time. This offer of friendliness, this meeting of a dear friend from the past so soon after disaster, was breaking all the rules.

"It's a pretty steep climb, dude," the man's voice said again.

Cecil finally climbed into the open back and took a seat on an Aztec type rug decorating the floor. "Kainalu? Really? It's been... I don't really know."

Kainalu turned back for just a moment as she drove the narrow road up the hill to safety. "I bet twenty-five years, at least. How have you been?"

The man sitting in the back offered him a burning cigarette that probably had little or no tobacco in it. Cecil politely waved it off, as well as Kainalu's question.

"That was..." Cecil paused at the thoughts sweeping across his mind. Stress was finally taking its toll on him. Fighting them back as best he could he began to feel his eyes watering. A few moments ago, angry residents were destroying his car and now his almost forgotten sweetheart from the old Makena hippie camps had picked him up.

"A long time ago," Kainalu finished for him. "I hear you're into land development these days." The tone of her voice stiffened a little at that.

Cecil refused to talk about it. He was stuck somewhere between extreme anger and exhausted surrender. Kainalu's voice had suddenly submerged his mind right back into those carefree days on that remote Maui beach. He was having what he would later recall as an epiphany of perspective.

"You said you're going to the Princeville fountain?"

"Yeah, dude," the man behind him said, offering him a smoke again. Cecil turned away.

"Will you join us?" Kainalu asked sweetly.

His heart skipped wildly. Those were the same words she had met him with, when she invited him and a friend to join them in that Maui beach commune. Cecil felt the tightness in his chest fade away almost instantly.

"Yes," Cecil said softly. Kainalu had probably been the only woman he had ever really loved. "Yes, I would love to. I'm feeling a lot better now."

It might have been the second-hand smoke, but he didn't think so.

~~~

The great eastern expanse of the dark Pacific had almost been crossed. The water had warmed considerably, both from the previous day's tropical sun and imperceptibly from this evening's gentle full moon. The earthquake pulse had been traveling nearly six hours now, and was a few dozen minutes from its first Hawaiian shoreline.

Six chanters and a guitar player stood in its path.

As some mystics would confirm, if asked, the sea's energy is a living entity, quite capable of perceiving its surroundings. As other mystics and many chanters would confirm, motivated voices could reach far beyond the simple acoustics their mouths might afford, and travel infinitely along paths human minds could direct.

Regardless, Onolani's sweet voice sang softly amongst her colleagues on the beach of Hanalei bay. The stars just above the horizon had moved an inch higher since they began their chants. Somewhere inside her, deep within a place she could never describe with simple spoken words, Onolani felt her voice finally reach the great pulse moving toward them all.

She swooned at the realization, felt Birdman's strong hand hold her steady and returned quickly to stand upright and focus - to greet the still distant visitor. Quickly, she let her trained consciousness take over, closing her eyes to see it better. There, in the dark, her bare feet within the very sea she sought to alter, she spoke to it of *the love*. An ancient love shared between the great forces of Earth and the appreciative peoples of men and women. She projected her love of living close to the sea, on an island so incredibly beautiful that destruction, by great waves, would be an extraordinary shame. She imagined idyllic images of beaches with children playing. She sent these and many thoughts forward to the great pulse, but soon had to pause. Such emotion was exhausting to communicate, and again she fell back onto Birdman.

"Are you OK, Ono?" Birdman whispered, but quickly saw she was deep within some kind of trance. His arms held her with patience.

Onolani slowly took a deep breath and exhaled silently.

Then she listened. Racing forward, between the surface of windblown waves down to the sandy reaches of the unfathomable depths below, the great pulse spoke.

It told her of how the planet must build constantly, resulting in her sometimes massive earthquakes. It told Onolani that the planet's very heart insisted the land grow higher as she sought to reach outside the atmosphere with her mountains. She saw the vast oceans of water and air as an irritation, constantly eroding the great peaks so that she must build them all over again. If she could reach beyond them both she would never decay. There she could kiss the stars with a perpetual clarity.

Onolani gasped at the vision, pushing back against Birdman's chest.

You, though, the pulse whispered, are one of us - the sea. You came from us; we can feel you tonight at our edges. The great planet sends us outward as she builds higher, but we are not her. Our love with people is indeed ancient and perpetual, but so is our mutual respect. Please forgive us, but we cannot assure your safety now. You must leave. You must not be surprised.

Onolani fell deeper into Birdman's arms. He sat his guitar down and checked his watch. 10:18. Ten minutes before the first wave was due to arrive.

"Time to go, Onolani."

The chanters had all stopped to listen to Onolani whisper in her trance and now, as she woke, they looked to her for guidance. Tears welled up in her eyes and she began to sob.

"Yes, we must go now."

~~~

Captain Tim double-checked his gear as Dave climbed into the glass bottom zodiac. Three days worth of food and water, solar panel for charging the cell phones and enough fuel to get to O'ahu if they needed to were all there. Fishing gear rounded out the emergency supplies. Dave's small tsunami buoy was ready to deploy at the mouth of the bay.

"You got a depth finder, right?" Dave asked for the seventh time.

He got a patient nod. "Push us off."

Dave loved being in a boat during a full moon. The way the water sparkled often tempted him to leave the world of rocks. The fast moving zodiac was leaving a trail of phosphorescence behind as they made for the deep waters outside the bay. Hanalei bay, under the famous Hanalei Moon, looked like a fairy tale from this perspective. Dave turned back to look out to sea. He hoped it would remain so.

Captain Tim's boat was too difficult to trailer out to high ground, so he, and dozens of other fishermen, were heading out to deep water where physics promised the wave wouldn't rise up. The lights of the flotilla were a mile ahead.

"600," Captain Tim announced, looking up from the depth finder. "We're safe from here on out."

Dave didn't breathe any easier, as he'd imagined he might have once they reached deep water. Neither did Captain Tim. Every fiber in their mortal bodies screamed at them to climb a mountain and not go out into the dark sea to face a tsunami.

Both men were betting their lives in the casino of science.

~~~

Pat, the cook from Tahiti Nui, John and his vivacious date, Taylor, all pulled up across the road from the Princeville fountain, next to a brightly colored Volkswagen van. Hundreds of people were dancing about the manicured lawn surrounding the thirty foot tall Neptune statue, with its pond like water feature. Loud music split the air, supported by dozens of hand drums.

"Party time!" Taylor screamed as she exited the truck. "Come on, Big John, let's get wild and dance!" She grabbed his hand and pulled him across the street.

Pat and the cook stopped in their tracks to watch as John glanced for a moment back at them, big grin on his face, and then turned to follow Taylor.

"Wow," Pat said with a large degree of wistfulness.

"Wow," the cook repeated. "I gotta get me one of those!"

Pat shook his head, seeking some rationalization. "I don't know; perfection is over-rated."

The cook laughed and looked at his boss for a long moment, then turned back toward the party. "Nah, you just haven't been here long enough."

~~~

Birdman noticed right away that as he, Onolani and the five other chanters in his car drove out of Hanalei toward the bridge, there was a distinct lack of headlights in his rear view mirrors.

"We're the last ones out of town," he remarked, not sure if that was a good thing or not. No cars were in front of them either.

It was quiet in the back, except for Onolani's gentle sobbing. The steep grade up the hill to Princeville was dark with only some red flares burning up ahead. A police cruiser, blue lights on but not flashing, blocked the lane back into the valley.

Birdman slowed down as he approached, so that he could pass the police blockade at a safe speed - then he noticed a hand held flashlight waving them on, quickly.

"Is he telling us to hurry?" Birdman asked.

"Sure looks like it," a voice from the back said. Onolani quieted and looked out at the flashlight.

Birdman unconsciously looked in his rear view mirror, half expecting to see something chasing them. Onolani caught his eye and quickly turned in her seat to look back as well.

As they got closer, the flashlight stopped waving them on and signaled them to stop.

An older officer walked up to their open window, caught a strong smell of something pungent in the air and pulled back a little, grinning. He shone his light into the back, confirming what he suspected.

"Hey, I think your car is smoking or something. Is it OK?"

Birdman glanced into the rear seat to see a chanter smoking one of those cigarettes that had little or no tobacco in it. Turning back to the officer he said, "No problem, probably just burning a little oil on the climb, sir."

The older officer laughed lightly at that. "Some sweet oil that must be." He looked down at his watch. "10:30 kids. You're a little late evacuating. The first wave got here two minutes ago..." Suddenly, he looked down the hill behind them, his face frozen.

Birdman, Onolani and the others all saw the officer's expression change from surprise to terror.

"Oh, my god!" the officer screamed. "Too late! Too late!" He turned and ran.

Everyone in Birdman's car turned to look, screaming and shrieking in the process. Birdman floored it. Of course, the old car took several moments to get going. But as they passed the older officer and the other two uniforms standing up ahead they saw them all laughing uproariously. The older officer looked at them, mimicked smoking a joint as they passed, then started laughing so hard he doubled over.

~~~

The pond surrounding Neptune at the Princeville fountain was full of people, mostly from Hanalei and mostly intoxicated. John had taken off his shirt, right before Taylor quickly wrestled him into the water, laughing and screaming and kissing him. He soon found someone willing to share a swing of tequila and found that it helped quite a bit. Helped put Taylor into perspective.

Pat and the Cook sat within view of his truck, but kept a good eye on the parade of human festivities all around them. Little children ran around playing and dancing, frantically trying to keep up with their hippie parents. Old people parked themselves a safe distance apart and clapped along with the drums.

Several intensely concerned people were kneeling in the open half-shell below Neptune, praying that he spare their neighborhoods. Others danced slowly around the supplicators as if they might propel the message higher. Everywhere smoke was rising from those cigarettes that had little or no tobacco in them.

Kainalu held Cecil's hand as she guided the both of them through the thickest part of the crowd, if for no other reason than to be in the middle of it all. A few people recognized the hated Maui developer, but since he was with Kainalu, they let him pass unimpeded.

Several worried mainland tourists, aware of the tsunami danger, stopped to ask about why people were having a party. Chad Pa, from the Tahiti Nui band *Island Fresh* took a moment to explain.

"If you're not having fun, it's your fault." He smiled. When they looked confused, he added, "So, go have some fun!"

Onolani and Birdman quickly broke the spell of the prank they had been subjected to and were dancing in the pond. There they found Trish in the pond, soaking wet and spinning wildly around, holding her hands high above her head.

When Trish saw her sister, she quickly stopped, smiling broadly under the influence of an intoxicating crowd. She kissed Onolani, hugged Birdman and swiftly made her way to dry land. Poi followed her, splashing and swimming as needed to follow her.

Finding a place several yards away from the crowd, Poi accepted the drying effects of Trish's fresh pareo as he snuggled against her leg where she sat. She was good dog-people. He had found an attentive spark in her personality that Onolani often directed elsewhere. Those long beach walks, sleeping at the foot of her bed and the way she cooked him bacon in the mornings all indicated that her life was moving in the right direction.

Poi moved up into Trish's lap, where he could better feel her heartbeat and lick her hand. Her eyes, when she looked at him like she was now, confirmed she was indeed ready. As she turned her beautiful face upward to gaze at the moon, he knew she was finally prepared to accept the great philosophy that he, Meher Baba, and all Jamaicans had been sent to Earth to spread: "Don't Worry, Be Happy."

twelve

~~~

Dawn brought many realities into perfect clarity.

The Princeville fountain would now always be considered the de facto tsunami-party venue of choice. Vegetarianism didn't protect you from tequila hangovers. Drum parties could hurt your hands if you played the entire set.

And, the tsunami was a non-event.

Dave, still cold from a night on the water, watched the sun rise from a National Guard helicopter that had been afforded to him by the Governor of Hawaii. As they lifted off slowly from the Princeville helipad the first rays of a warming, benevolent sun caught the mountain peaks above Hanalei. Dave only caught it in a glance, but quickly ignored his paperwork and turned back to watch the show.

The helicopter moved like smooth animation up and above the infinitely gorgeous landscape below. Slowly revolving around completely as they climbed, Dave enjoyed the very stuff of any flier's dreams. The young pilot, Lt. Gavin Tomlinson, inspired with some kind of theatric confidence found only in genius, danced along the treetops, sweeping high, then turning low, sometimes circling in pause. All of it accompanied by the most exquisite compressions enjoyed only in measured flight.

Dave looked down into his coffee and wondered if it might be spiked. It most likely wasn't. This was something entirely different.

Call it a contact high, or maybe it was a blessing. Whatever it might be, he was coming to a realization that the natural world, which he studied for a living, had a special quality quite beyond numbers, measurements and predictions. It was actually kind of cute. Not puppy dog cute but rather like young and knock-out gorgeous cute. It was vibrant, full of life, rambunctious. It was also whispering his name, with promises of adventure.

Embarrassed that he was feeling sexually attracted to an island, he quickly broke that train of thought. There was actually some work to be done. He began studying the coastline as they moved along Hanalei bay, tracing the contour out to the corner and then moving along toward the Na Pali coast.

From what he could see so far, there was no damage whatsoever. Debris lines were no farther than the last high tide's. Signaling the pilot to turn around, back toward Hanalei, Dave could see that the waves had been completely non-destructive. But there was one topographic feature that could still amplify any wave event. River mouths.

As they approached Hanalei town, and passed it going east toward the Hanalei River, both the pilot and Dave quickly noticed the inundated taro fields. All of the dikes had been crested just along the river. The bridge was dripping wet. And there in the middle of one taro field was what looked like a black Mercedes sitting perfectly upright on its nose.

~~~

Hanalei returned to normal except that coffee sales and ibuprofen sales were unusually high. All the tourists were happy their expensive vacations had not been ruined. They began shopping and exploring the beaches and waterfalls early. The residents slept in or skipped work altogether, those who could. The chickens, roosters included, seemed to have exhausted themselves during the night and were unusually absent from the background vibe. Good fortune was reflected up into a blue-bird sunny day with gentle tradewinds. One could taste an island-wide sense of relief. It tasted like victory.

UPS took a full half hour to unload all the new t-shirt boxes to the Tahiti Nui. Pat immediately tore open one box, grabbed a XXL short sleeve and hung it over the bar. Finally, Tahiti Nui had t-shirts again. Lots of them.

John was rudely awakened several times after 11:00 A.M. with beachfront owners wanting to list their properties. Fed up with the tropics, they had had their last tsunami scare. While on the third call, he made coffee and walked a large mug over to Taylor, who promptly vomited in the nearby trash can. Again.

Captain Tim hung a CLOSED sign on the mango tree where he normally picked up passengers for the ride to Kalalau. The glass bottom zodiac was getting a much needed rest. The new hammock suspending his sleepy head worked hard with the sun to keep his eyes in the shade.

Island Fresh had to rejuvenate. The boys in the band had played all night. Many of the guest drummers in the crowd would need weeks for their hands to return to normal. The Princeville maintenance people were fishing bikini tops and pareos out of the pond, recovering cell phones and slippers and planting sod back into the lawn. The guys at the police station were still telling the story about scaring the stoned hippies.

Onolani remembered how easily sleep came when you stayed up all night. It had been a while, but the peaceful sink into dreams was amazingly pleasant. She tried to project gratitude out to the great pulse, to the sea, but drifted off before she could muster the energy.

Birdman had a job. As much as he wanted to sleep he wanted more to never waste an opportunity to stack bananas, breadfruit, boxes and cans. It gave him time to think, uninterrupted by jungled mountains and blue skies.

~~~

Kainalu's brightly painted Volkswagen van made its way all around Princeville, picking up people to go back into Hanalei. She then turned into the parking area of the new *Tastes Like Chicken* cafe.

Cecil waved meekly and walked up toward the already open sliding door. The coffee hadn't helped, but he thought the four egg omelet might have. He had still not figured out how they could keep their prices so low.

With everyone on board they made their way down the hill and into Hanalei valley. When they came to the bridge they paused. No one said anything as they stared at the black Mercedes sticking straight up into the air.

"Unbelievable," Kainalu whispered, a little louder than she had hoped.

Cecil didn't say anything, but didn't shirk from the consolatory pat on his back from the guy behind him.

~~~

Trish slept fitfully in the warm morning, dodging the sun's intrusion through the windows as best she could. Each time she awoke, she noticed the roosters were mercifully silent. Yet now there seemed to be a large pig snoring close by. Seeing Poi on his back again, she turned him over. The large pig became quiet.

She would have forced herself up earlier, but today held a decision she was hesitant to make. Hoping that staying in bed would allow some miraculous solution to appear seemed a good strategy.

~~~

Before Dave could finally get some sleep, he had a report to generate. The State Civil Defense office had insisted on an early analysis, and if possible, a hint at his interpretation of any new tsunami lines.

After consulting with the San Diego office of the U.S. Geological Service, running more scenarios on his computer and adjusting for the data from this latest event, he had more than a hint to give them.

He emailed the analysis right away, but added under his signature a note.

"Will send my final report on updated tsunami inundation lines tomorrow morning. If you want them sooner, come to Tahiti Nui tonight."

~~~

Pat walked into the bar right before sunset, just in time for those last rays to announce how loud the colors of his new aloha shirt were. He whispered to the bartender that all drinks tonight were free and walked outside to stand under the Tahiti Nui marquee.

An approaching group of fat tire bicycles approached just as he swung his ukulele into action.

The group of school teachers, traveling together and enjoying a bike ride, immediately noticed the tall, colorful character by the road, singing. Pulling over they soon surrounded him and joined in to *Hanalei Moon*.

That attracted several other people driving by and soon the Tahiti Nui parking lot was full for the second time in its history.

~~~

A tequila sunrise late in the day had revived Taylor enough to the point where she could accompany John to Tahiti Nui.

"Big announcement tonight," John said. "The geologist guy is announcing his findings on the tsunami inundation lines." He was unusually animated.

Taylor rubbed her forehead deeply with both palms.

"Is that all?"

John was dancing around his beachfront home now, spinning and playing some air-guitar version of *Stairway to Heaven* only he could hear.

"Nope," he said emphatically. "That's not the only news!"

Taylor was feeling better, finally. A swim in the ocean and a hot shower plus the new clothes John had bought her all combined to make her feel a little frisky. That, and watching John dance. He was silly, but she loved the way he played air guitar, like he used to be in a band or something, she thought.

"Big day, babe," John sang, pulling into a guitar riff.

Taylor walked up to him, propelled by the same urge that had drawn her to him initially. Putting her arms around his neck, she lightly kissed his lips.

"How big, John?" She smiled seductively and pushed into him slightly.

Undeterred for the moment, John grinned. "Those three beachfront mansions I listed this morning? You know, the guys that are fed up with tsunami evacuations?"

"Yes," Taylor said, pulling him slowly over toward the massive leather couch.

"Well, I just sold every one of them!"

Taylor knew that meant a lot of money. But, she could see it really meant her squeeze was exceedingly happy, and that meant she might soon be herself.

"To who?" She had him sitting on the couch now, right next to her bare legs.

"Three different Canadian buyers from the Queen Charlotte Islands area. They're fed up with all the earthquakes..."

At that precise moment John lost his train of thought as Taylor directed it elsewhere.

~~~

Tahiti Nui was already packed by the time Dave got there. Making his way through the throng of bodies, some already dancing, he found Pat up on stage singing and playing his ukulele still. This time, though, he had a bass guitar backup and someone on harmonica.

The bartender waved him over.

"You're the geologist guy, right?" she asked.

"Does that mean I get a free drink?"

"Actually, it does. But there's someone been waiting for an hour for you to show up."

Dave knew that people didn't go to bars to wait for handsome geologists to just *show up*. They either had a rock they wanted identified or they wanted to kick his ass for a recommendation he had made. He looked around the bar for trouble. In a moment he saw the same professional girl from before, still young *and* unfairly beautiful.

"That's her," the bartender confirmed, following his gaze.

She made a beeline for Dave, catching his arm before he could flee the packed bar.

"Come with me, I won't bite."

"Unless I pay extra?" Dave said, following reluctantly toward a corner away from most of the crowd.

She laughed. "No, I never use my teeth." She turned, looked him the eye and added. "Ever."

"Look..." Dave tried to say before she put her finger against his lips.

"Don't worry, big geologist boy. I'm not here to seduce your opinion on some tsunami lines or whatever that is. I got paid to try and that gig is over." She smiled about as authentically as a professional girl might be expected to. "OK?"

Dave nodded, noticing how close she insisted on standing to him. He looked around for the local lady, dressed in many yards of fabric, so expansive was her beauty. She wasn't there.

"I hear you're going to announce your findings tonight." She let her hand follow his hairline back to his ear.

"Yes, and I think I should go do just that, right now!"

"Wait," she purred. "I have something for you."

Dave closed his eyes as he watched her hand descend between them. It would be far too embarrassing if she actually...

"Here," she whispered, placing something into his hands.

Immediately, Dave knew what it was and smiled.

"These are red," she said. "Collect the entire series, if you like." Leaning over to kiss him on the cheek, she added. "I've always had a thing for scientists."

With that, she moved away from him, his back still stuck against the wall. Blowing a kiss she disappeared to the other side of the bar.

Dave looked down into his hands, glanced around the bar quickly and then slipped the panties into his right pocket, atop the blue ones.

~~~

Onolani needed to get out of the house soon. She had just woken up as the sun disappeared. Birdman had told her he was going straight to bed after work. So it was her and Tahiti Nui. Until she saw Trish and Poi returning from their late afternoon beach walk.

"Sis!"

"Ono!"

"Poi!"

"Bark bark!"

"Come with me to Tahiti Nui," Onolani said, a big pout on her face. "My man is sleeping. Can you imagine that?"

Trish gave her a big thumbs up as she stood in the concrete basin of water. The sand slowly fell off her feet as she wiggled her toes. After drying them off and climbing the stairs, she turned to look for Poi.

"Poi!" Trish called. "Will Poi be OK by himself?" Trish asked her sister, looking around.

They both saw him prancing over to the house next door. He turned when Trish called and wagged his butt furiously. In his mouth was a very large, dead but perfectly sun-toasted crab.

~~~

"Ladies, gentlemen and everyone in between," Dave announced over the stage microphone. The crowd, though, was simply too large to calm with one simple sentence.

Unless you were Captain Tim. He walked up onto stage and simply stood next to Dave, his arms crossed. Almost instantly the crowd quieted and began to turn, facing the stage. Dave looked over and tried to figure what this secret magnetism was that Captain Tim possessed. It might have been the finely tailored Jimmy Buffet style clothing, or the impossibly white Panama hat. His face was finely chiseled with weather and adventure. Dave looked closer, thinking for a moment he might have found it - the man's mustache seemed to have been stolen from Tom Selleck himself.

"Mahalo," Captain Tim said. "Let's give the nice geologist man our attention please." The microphone a few feet off to his side, without needing him to speak into it, amplified his voice out of pure respect. A young backpacker girl from Vermont bounded up to him with a Gibley's Gin and Tonic in a lead glass tumbler, handing it up on bended knee.

Dave stood a bit dumbfounded as the Captain stepped down into yet another throng of fame-worshipping backpackers.

"OK, everyone, my name is David Lesperance..."

"Yeah, we got that last time!" a voice boomed from the back.

Dave cringed for a second, until everyone started clapping. People sitting at the bar, stood up and clapped as well. The bartender rang the ship's bell. Pat leaned against the kitchen doorway smoking a cigar and blowing the smoke back to where the fans could suck it outside. Cheers were going out and a chant of "Geology Rocks!" got started for a moment.

The crowd approached the stage like a Rolling Stones concert was about to start. There in the very front of the mass of people was his professional friend, the young *and* beautiful girl with a taste in colorful underwear. She opened and offered up a Hinano beer.

Dave leaned over and said, above as much of the clapping as he could. "Sometimes, I just can't say no," and took the bottle from her hands.

She mouthed silently back to him, "I know."

~ ~ ~

Onolani and Trish were stuck outside on the deck, unable to squeeze in toward the bar. They could see the geologist guy up on stage about to talk.

"What do you want to do?" Trish asked.

"I want to get to the bar," Onolani said. "Follow me, closely."

Trish watched in horrified fascination as her sister went up to everyone blocking her way and squeezed their butts. Men, women, it didn't matter. As each surprised patron turned around, they saw Onolani and Trish move quickly past them. Soon, they were within ordering range of the bartender.

"OK, folks," Dave began again. "Thank you so much for the warm welcome, but I must ask, how do you know I will be giving out good news tonight?" He quickly realized he might have tipped his hand already and added, "Or not?"

"If you weren't, you would have fled town!" a voice yelled from near the bar.

Everyone cheered at that. Dave nodded. Difficult logic to argue against. And quite true.

"Well, then," Dave looked down at his notes. "You are correct!"

Another loud cheer went up in the bar, this time Pat put the cigar in his teeth and clapped as well. The cook was dancing in celebration back in the kitchen, still closely watching the broccoli steam.

"My recommendation to the State of Hawaii Civil Defense will be limited to only one small change in the maps."

The crowd got quiet, thinking there would be no change at all, especially after a tsunami had come and gone with no effect.

"All tsunami inundation lines in effect are still valid, except for those around the mouth of the Hanalei River..."

Cheers and whistles drowned out his voice. Kainalu, sipping a root beer out near the road was listening intently. Cecil had asked her to.

He was incapable of leaving his vacation rental at the moment, paralyzed with dread about the ruling and afraid to confront any drivers of large pickup trucks he might meet there.

Dave held up his hands for attention. Captain Tim took a step toward the stage and everyone calmed down.

"Except for the mouth of the Hanalei River," Dave continued. "And up river five hundred yards, with a buffer on either side of three hundred yards. Those dimensions will be included in a new no-build zone. Otherwise, everything is the same." He pulled out his phone and emailed this recommendation to the Governor himself. He was now officially off the clock.

The bartender was ringing the ship's bell furiously now, girls were dancing barefoot on the bar and the noise was stupefying. Kainalu wrote down what she heard, made a couple of phone calls and then got back on her bicycle to visit Cecil.

Dave stepped down off the stage, successfully avoiding the professional girl, hoping he could now escape the bar. However, he was quickly surrounded by other adoring fans.

"Can we get your autograph?"

Dave looked at the group of three young ladies and smiled.

"We're big science fans!"

"Sure, uh, where do I sign?" Dave smiled.

The first girl handed him a magic marker, turned and pulled her spandex pants down a few inches, exposing just the top of what appeared to Dave to be the most perfect gluteus maximus he had ever seen.

"Really, on your butt?"

She wiggled it a little as her two friends laughed.

"Yes! Of course!"

Dave could hear chants of "Free Drinks! Free Drinks!" in the background as he narrowed his focus to writing his name as slowly on her skin as possible. Naturally, he had to hold onto her hips to keep his pen steady.

"Me next!" the second girl demanded.

"Why not?" Dave beamed. "What are you girls up to?"

"We're hiking out to Kalalau in a couple of days, after our yoga retreat is over."

Dave looked at the three ladies a little closer. They were all in fantastic shape, all wearing spandex like they had invented it and were its chief salespersons.

"Yoga, eh?" Dave commented as he signed the second girl's hard belly, right below her navel.

"Yes, indeed," the third girl confirmed. "Nude yoga."

Dave saw his pen waver and fall into the well of her belly button.

"That's OK," she said softly. "It'll wash off in the waterfalls."

"Nude yoga," Dave repeated. "That must be something." He didn't dare try and describe the visuals racing through his mind.

"Sure is," the third girl said, moving up close to him for her autograph. She pulled down her tube top until it only covered the essential zone. "By invitation only..."

Dave looked up into her hazel eyes and grinned broadly. "Really? So, how does one get invited to such a thing?"

"Oh, that's easy," the first girl said, thrusting her hips to one side so she could inspect his signature. "All you need to do is prove you can sign your name, three times."

"Two down, one to go, Mister handsome geologist stud," the third girl said. "First name on my right one, last name on my left one, if you please."

Dave now understood why on his helicopter tour this very morning he had felt the seduction of nature. Here were three of its finest emissaries, ready to take him on an adventure. And they were indeed young and knock-out gorgeous cute, just as his daydream had hinted.

After the signing was done, and they had retired to the bar, the first girl snuggled up to Dave while the other two were on his right.

"So, do all you sexy scientist types always carry a pocket protector around?" All three of them giggled. Dave almost joined them.

"No, darling, but I've got lots of protection."

thirteen

~~~

Trish waited a couple of days before deciding to tell her sister. In fact, she waited until the morning of the day before she intended to leave for Chicago. Unfortunately, the island sensed her departure and was currently throwing everything it had at her, in an attempt to keep her.

She had decided to hike out to Hanakapiai beach, the first on the Kalalau trail, for her last site-seeing adventure. As she soon found out, it was a huge mistake. She should have hung out at the Costco food court.

The valleys of the Na Pali coastline were more beautiful than the pictures had indicated. After a few minutes she simply put her camera in her day pack, unable to take another shot of blue skies, green jungle and cobalt colored water. How many postcards could a girl use anyhow?

Eventually making it to the beach, crossing the stream and settling in for lunch, she sat quietly. Turtles swarmed the small waves cresting just offshore, occasionally riding a gentle wave all the way into the cream colored sand. They reminded her of Poi, except that perhaps they weren't as cute.

The warm sun she would probably miss the most, but maybe it was the sweet air sweeping softly out of the valley behind her. Scents of pikake moved among others of guava. She looked up into the few small clouds hitching a ride on the wind, carefree as to their destination.

Turning back to her bottle of water she noticed movement at the trail coming into the valley. Other than these new people and her, the entire beach was empty. No footprints, no sounds, no one else to appreciate it all.

She watched as the three young women and a man descended the few steps down, crossed the stream while laughing and splashing each other and then climbed back up onto her side of the beach.

Trish wanted them to act as if she were having a private moment, leaving her to a few moments of contemplation. No. They walked right up to her and introduced themselves, full of that special quality of conversation international backpackers all embrace.

"Good morning," the first girl said. "Beautiful, isn't it?" She sat her backpack on the sand close to Trish and turned to the others. "Hey, there are turtles!"

Trish turned to watch as her friends approached. The guy looked a little familiar, but it was difficult to tell. His smile was so big it deformed his normal features.

"Time to swim!" the second girl yelled, dropping her pack next to the first one and taking off her shoes.

The water did look inviting, Trish had to admit. But she specifically was avoiding the ocean now. Something told her that if she entered she would never be let go. Nothing dark like a drowning, but rather like a baptism. The sparkling light on the water was whispering on behalf of the island. "Submerge yourself here now and your soul will forever be with us."

Trish watched the group prepare to swim and wondered if they were going to change into their swimsuits, right out in the open. She noticed one of the girls had something scrawled across her impossibly tight belly, in ink. They didn't seem to be pulling swimsuits out of their backpacks...

Suddenly, it became obvious there were to be no swimsuits wasted on this adventure. All three women were soon naked, folding up their hiking clothes neatly and laying it on top of their packs.

"Coming with?" The girl with ink on the tops of her breasts asked.

Trish shook her head no. Surely, if she went swimming with these gorgeous women, the shark would leave them alone and get her first.

"Healing waters, these are," the first girl noted to no one in particular, watching the turtles frolic. The other two had already run into the surf, laughing and shouting.

"Healing?" Trish had to ask. She suspected something mystical with every nook and cranny of this island. The ocean should be no different.

"Not just for your body, either," she said looking at Trish.

"What do you mean?"

The girl, quite confident in her nakedness in front of a stranger, smiled but didn't offer an explanation.

"Just look at our expressions when we come back out," she said, slipping on some goggles. "You'll understand then."

She walked half way to the wet sand before turning and yelling back at the last of their group.

"Hey, Dave! Are you coming in or what?"

Dave had already folded his clothes as well, but had been distracted by heavy concentrations of silica in the basalt rock near the caves.

"Here I come!" he yelled like a little kid, running full bore up to the surf and then stopping at the edge.

Trish noticed his tan stopped at his waist, unlike his hiking buddies. The girls were egging him on as he held his arms toward the sky, waited for a small wave and then dove in.

All four of them played like kids, splashing, diving and apparently taking turns kissing Dave.

Trish finally picked up her stuff, threw her pack on her shoulder and crossed the stream to return to Ke'e beach and Onolani's parked car. She looked with some considerable sadness high up into the cloud shrouded valley, letting the cool breeze soften the warmth of the sun on her shoulders. It wasn't going to change her mind now. This island had tried to seduce her, but she was going to win. Turning to look back at the beach, and the four hikers enjoying the water, she now had her escape justified. It was now obvious, she felt, that paradise was for the young.

~~~

Poi was up with the dawn the next morning. He sniffed around the large suitcase for a good twenty minutes, trying to figure out what it was. Onolani didn't have one, nor did any of the people that visited. Except for Trish. It had disappeared quickly on her arrival, but now it had been poised by the door all night, standing upright and looking very much out of place.

The screen door opened silently as Poi was distracted by the seams and the zippers of the black monolith.

"Poi boy," Kainalu whispered. "Is anyone up yet?" She reached down and picked him up, rubbing behind his ears as she entered the kitchen to start coffee.

"Your friend is leaving," she said softly, kissing his head. "That is her suitcase." She set him on the punee and walked back to the kitchen.

Poi was very concerned now. First there was the black monolith that smelled faintly of Trish but more like things far away. And, now, Kainalu, almost as easy to read as a cat with her body language, was sad, almost depressed.

"You're going to have take extra good care of Onolani, you know."

Poi watched her talk, watched her eye movements, her lips, but mostly her hands.

"She's going to be sad, maybe cry a lot..."

Poi saw her hands move up to her eyes for a moment. This was really bad, he thought.

Finally, the coffee smells filled the room. A door opened in the hallway. Poi jumped down off the punee, took the corner into the hallway a little too fast. His little butt, sitting atop such powerful legs, could not weigh down his momentum and he slid into the wall.

"Oh, Poi!" Trish almost cried. She picked him up and walked back into the TV room. "I'm going to really, really miss you, little guy."

Between Kainalu and Trish showing their emotions, Poi knew trouble was definitely afoot. All he could do was appeal to her good sense, and lick her face. That worked for his cat friend next door, the mynah bird with the broken wing and Onolani. Surely, Trish would see the wisdom of it as well.

"Is your sister up yet?" Kainalu asked.

Trish took a deep breath. "No, she's not coming to the airport. Said it was the saddest place on Earth, and didn't want to have anything to do with it."

"Yeah," Kainalu said, looking down into her coffee. "I've heard that, too."

Neither spoke while Trish made her coffee. The sun was creeping down the distant mountain peaks, trying one last time to convince her to stay. She dropped her gaze, avoiding the windows.

"Is this your only bag?" Kainalu took the handle. "I'll go ahead and load it up. Take your time."

"I'll come on down, too," Trish said quickly.

"No," Kainalu said, looking down at Poi. His tail was trying to wag just a little but it was a big effort. "Take your time with Poi, you know, saying goodbye." She turned and wheeled the suitcase out the door.

Poi turned to look up at Trish. He had seen the look in her eyes at the tsunami party, certain that she had received the message. What could possibly change that? He walked hesitantly up to her feet, licked her toes once, and peered up again, hoping to see a change in her eyes.

They were still sad, but now were full of tears.

~~~

The drive into the Lihue airport was silent. Kainalu didn't offer up any conversation and Trish refused to look out the window. It wasn't until they got close that Kainalu finally said something.

"I've got to get some gas, if you don't mind. I think we're a bit early, anyhow."

Trish nodded. When they finally stopped at the pumps she looked up. Costco gas. A little bile moved up into her throat in disgust. The long tentacles of the mainland way of life were pulling at her already. First they stealthily crept into her mind, reminding her she wasn't from here, telling her she had a job, a career to maintain - telling her paradise wasn't for a girl from Chicago. Now, it was assaulting her nose with the smell of gasoline, the torture of high intensity lighting and generically bland design.

Kainalu soon got back in and started the car. She looked at Trish, who was still keeping her head down.

"I'm sorry," Kainalu said.

The question, sorry for what, hung in Trish's mind for a full minute, until they stopped at a red light. There she saw a group of colorful chickens gathered under a tree. It might have even been the same ones she had seen when Onolani had first picked her up.

"Sorry for what, Kainalu?"

Kainalu didn't answer for a moment, steering around a couple of roosters insisting on standing their ground, or asphalt as the case might be. She remained silent for the next four minutes getting to the airport.

She pulled up to the simple airline counters, a few steps from the curve, put the car into park and jumped out. Trish opened her door and went for her bag. Kainalu was wrestling it out of the trunk.

"Thank..." Trish tried to say just as Kainalu gave her a big enveloping hug. As most people she had met on Kauai were prone to do, she hugged a moment longer than Trish was comfortable with.

"I'm sorry," Kainalu finally answered as she turned to climb back into her car. "For leaving you at the saddest place on Earth."

~~~

Poi sat at the bottom of the stairs to Hale Ha Ha O'Hanalei. All day. From there he figured he could see if she came out of the house, or tried to go in. The cat from next door spied on him several times, but left him alone. She could tell.

A mynah bird, nearly exhausted from squawking with his siblings, rested in the shade of the plumeria tree between the house and the school. It watched Poi pacing back and forth, but finally had to fly away, unable to watch the sad scene a moment longer.

Thinking it might somehow make her materialize from thin air, Poi walked into the concrete water basin and splashed a little. He looked all around, even up into the sky. Nothing.

Dejected, he walked slowly over to the patch of red dirt where the happy rainbow children played, hoping he could absorb some of their energy. No one was outside playing yet. Recess was still an hour away. He laid down in the dirt anyhow. Resting his head down on his front paws, he felt his first tear ever slide down his furry nose.

~~~

The Tradewinds Air gate was the farthest from the security screening area. Fortunately, that was only three gates down. Trish had checked her one bag, and with only her small pack to carry, she walked casually toward it.

She noticed that this was one of the quietest airports she had ever been in. No music was piped into speakers hidden cleverly away. No announcements were being made. No airplanes were on the runway, and amazingly enough, none were at the gates. The place looked deserted. Except for the passengers sitting around.

At her gate there were about forty or fifty people. No one was talking. Most people had ear-buds in, already absorbed into their favorite form of escapism. Several, though, were standing up next to the floor-to-ceiling windows, looking out. A few had their hands flat against the glass, as if they were trying to listen. Several children were crying, not hysterically, as children often do in the vicinity of airplanes, but softly. Sobbing into their mother's arms, or their fathers. In one corner two very young sisters were sobbing into each other's arms.

An elderly man, an agent for Tradewinds, was carrying a box with him, handing out Kleenex to people. Even those that seemed preoccupied with something took the time to look up at him, nod thanks and take a packet. As he gave his last packets to two more crying children, he patted their heads and turned to get more. Trish watched him closely. His eyes were watery as he passed her.

That's when the first delay announcement was made.

~~~

When the second delay announcement was made, Trish began to worry. Her direct flight to San Francisco with a connection to Chicago was now three hours behind. That meant a scramble in SFO for a new connecting flight. Finally, two agents came into the boarding area, asking people if they wanted to go to Honolulu first. There was room on the Honolulu to San Francisco flight for about twenty people.

Trish raised her hand. She had to get off the island immediately. Already, she could sense it was making escape difficult. Here at the boarding gate, she couldn't avoid the huge picture windows, all of which were simply servants of the gods of light and reflection. The blue sea, just off the end of the runway, looked inviting. Too inviting. Windows on the opposite side of the gate showed hints of the backside of the mountains above Hanalei, and she knew what they held. Her heart. At least they did until she could get away from here. Distance would save her.

Walking into the empty restroom to freshen up, she took a moment to look into her own eyes. They were clearer than she could ever remember. The red veins she'd thought were permanent had faded. And her skin color had a nice hint of brown, banishing the whitewash of winter. Her boring hair now had streaks of sun enhanced lightness. She was looking like she belonged here, maybe in a hammock with a cool tropical smoothie, watching the colors in the sky compete with those in the ocean...

Her daydream paused. Ah... there it was, again. It was creeping into her mind once more, insidious and clever. The Island. Trish blinked, stepping away from the mirror for a moment. Such powers were impressive, and exactly why she needed to flee. She was losing control. She turned away and made for the exit.

An old lady was entering. Immediately, she smiled broadly at Trish, putting out her hand, pointing at Trish's face.

"Sorry, honey," she said. Her voice was friendly, but had an ancient tone to it. "You've got a little... well, just there on your forehead."

"Oh!" Trish reached up. "Thanks." She wiped above her brow.

The old lady frowned. "Still there. I suggest the mirror."

At the mention of the mirror, Trish paused. No. No way, the mirror was dangerous now. It was The Island's tool, attempting to trick her into staying, to trap her.

The old lady stood there, her grin morphing into a concerned smile. Trish shook off the hallucination, thanked her and turned to return to the sink, and mirror.

She looked again. Nothing was on her forehead, perhaps it had fallen away, whatever it was. Habitually, she studied herself again, her reflection. Pursing her lips, raising her eyebrows, tilting her head left, then right. Every little thing she always did. She *was* in control!

It was amazing, though, she noted. Her sun kissed skin actually had a nice glow to it. She leaned in a little closer, looked a little deeper into the glass. She blinked once, twice, but it wasn't her focus. Something was really... appearing.

There, just under the surface of a couple of extra decades, she could see herself. Young and beautiful. Happy. Running carefree, perhaps into the ocean at Hanakapiai beach...

Quickly, she stood back from the mirror, tearing her eyes away.

"Damn!" she muttered.

She washed her hands again, went to the paper towel dispenser, pulling four of them out. Turning to look around, she noticed the restroom was still empty. Where was that old lady?

Freaked out a little by the visions, and at a new thought that was now bouncing around in her mind, Trish bent down and looked under the three stall doors. No feet.

Quickly, she walked out into the bordering area. Scanning the thinning crowd, she saw no one over sixty. Fearing she might actually be losing her mind, she walked over to the sundry shop. No old lady. The coffee kiosk attendant had seen no one by that description. She turned and looked at the TSA screening folks. No, she wouldn't bother them. They were probably bored and might want to quiz her about her psychological status.

Sitting down, she put her head down into her hands and closed her eyes.

"You've got big mojo," Trish whispered. "I'll give you that."

Maybe it was her alcohol withdrawal that was causing the hallucinations - she tried to rationalize. She had never been that big of a drinker though. Or maybe she had eaten some kind of tropical fruit that had such qualities, although she had never heard of such a thing. Or, maybe, she feared, there were such things as Island spirits. At least these were nice Island spirits. Tenacious Island spirits that...

"Trish Nojes! Trish Nojes!"

... that know my name! She looked up, incredulous. This was getting a bit spooky.

"Trish Nojes, Gate 6 immediately, for departure!" The PA system clicked off right after the audible exasperation of an overworked gate agent.

Running as fast as she could, as if something might really be chasing her, she made the jet-way just as they closed the door. The smaller jet that would take her to Honolulu had one seat left, by a window.

Of course. It was trying one last time. She closed the window shade just as the plane pushed back from the gate.

~~~

She daydreamed of magic.

Onolani was sitting at the bay on a large red and yellow blanket in the dancing shade of a coconut palm. Her eyes didn't leave the sea, even as Birdman approached and sat quietly next to her. Neither of them talked.

Poi had followed Birdman from the house and quickly curled up next to Onolani's bare feet. He tried to lick her toes, to let her know it was going to be OK, but she moved them away. He curled up again, but this time sat still. He could tell. She would need time.

Poi's wet tongue between her toes broke her trance. The daydream was quickly swallowed by regret. It had been a mistake not to take her sister to the airport, a selfish mistake, Onolani thought. She was angry at her for leaving on such short notice. No. Disappointed. Crushed was perhaps a better word. Onolani debated the adjectives as she fought to control the growing negative energy from ruining her mood entirely.

Having trained her mind for years on just how to do this, she began by taking a slow, deep breath of the ocean air. The warmth entered her nose, her mouth, and swept into her lungs. She held it there for several moments, quite filled for a moment, then exhaled slowly... into emptiness. Years of training also told her something else. She would need time.

Poi and Birdman watched her closely. The little dog snuggled a bit closer, trying as hard as he could to give her toes some warmth without disturbing her focus. The aging hippie picked up the beat when she began a second deep breath and began playing. Soft, mellow, slack-key notes floated around them all from his acoustic beach guitar.

Onolani reached out for her two men, Poi at her feet and Birdman by her side. This was what she had wanted to share with her sister, this bond with other loving creatures, anchored in a magical place.

~~~

As the small jet began descending Trish slid up the window shade.

Honolulu was a shock.

Concrete sprouted from every open pore in the overwhelmed land. Lines of cars appeared parked on the main roads and the suburbs reached high up into the mountain valleys and ridges. It was far larger than she had imagined.

She had skipped it when arriving on Kauai, and now was grateful for that small favor. It would have spoiled the fantasy.

Another Tradewinds agent was standing just outside their arrival gate, holding up a sign that said "SFO". Trish got to the small crowd just as they were announcing a delay until tomorrow morning.

"Are you kidding?" One of the passengers closest to the agent was waving his hands.

"We will provide transportation to a hotel, two meal vouchers, and we'll pick you up in the morning."

Most of the crowd grumbled. The four that didn't started smiling at each other. They looked like backpackers, a few years off their youth, but quite energized now. One of them turned, saw Trish and smiled, giving her a thumbs up.

He was cute in the way a freshman is to a senior. Trish smiled back.

"We're going to La Mariana for a drink. Come with us," the freshman offered.

His friends turned to her now. They looked like a fun bunch, unlike most strangers, unlike ax murderers or bad apples. For some strange reason they reminded her of an older version of the backpackers she had met on Kauai.

"Is it close by?" Trish asked, stepping closer to the group.

"Right under the airport's departure path..."

"Very close!" One of the girls laughed.

The freshman leaned over a little closer. "Best strawberry-banana smoothie in a Tiki Bar this side of Tiwaka's."

"Can we cab it?" Trish asked.

~ ~ ~

"You ever heard of Aikana Land Group?"

Cecil perked up at the question.

"Sure." He looked up from his cocktail. The view there was boring him anyhow. It had been a day since Kainalu had given him the news. Ever since then, she had been on the phone, and he had been in the scotch.

"Good," Kainalu said. "They're the biggest private land investor in the State. My cousin on the haole side of the family owns it."

Cecil liked the sound of all of that.

"Jesse says he'll trade your hundred acres of condemned taro patch for one acre of desert on the south side," Kainalu stood up with her arms crossed. She had brokered an offer, and felt proud.

Cecil frowned. "One acre of desert?"

Kainalu smiled, having let the hook sink in. "Yes. On the ocean. In Poipu. You know, the *resort*." She didn't often stray from her more laid back personality, but when there was a chance to save her neighborhood, she summoned up old skill sets.

"That might be some pretty sweet desert," Cecil echoed, rubbing his chin.

"It is. Jesse needs some wetlands he can donate to the State in exchange for a deal he has to make on Lana'i. Believe me, he's making out better on this deal than you are." Kainalu walked up to Cecil and playfully put her finger on his chest. "You should take the deal."

Cecil gave her a friendly hug. Besides being grateful he noticed it felt like the right thing to do. That forced a pause, and he made a mental note - he might be softening up. He would have to keep an eye on that.

"I might just take that deal, let's go have a look at it," Cecil said, beaming. He walked out to the lanai of his vacation rental. There, just under a small cap of white clouds, the great mountain peaks looked down at him. Maybe this was better. He nodded toward them.

"You know, Kainalu," Cecil turned to look at her, feeling full of confidence again. "I don't always win... but, I never lose."

~~~

The quick seven minute ride to La Mariana took a route that was never within sight of more than 5% of nature at any time. Overhead freeway lanes blocked the sky. Warehouses took over after that.

"Sorry," the freshman said. "It looks like a bad movie, but this bar was here before all of this."

"At least it's on the water," one of the girls in the group offered. "And there's even a marina there."

"Oldest Tiki bar on the island. You know, a classic spot." The freshman smiled just like he did the first time, with some kind of hypnotic rise of his eyebrows. It was captivating her.

Trish smiled back, but looked away quickly. He might not be just a cute freshman. He might move up to sexy sophomore if he kept this up. She recognized, though, that it was dangerous to let her mind wander this way, there was no window shade she could enlist.

"Here we are!" the girls chimed.

They had been right, of course. An oasis in the desert. La Mariana was a classic 1950's style Tiki bar, complete with hanging glass balls, situated next to a private, twenty-slip marina. The crowd of four people already there smiled as they walked in, then went back to their Mai Tais.

Sitting down at a rope encircled table, the freshman followed Trish around the table as everyone scooted in.

"I never buy a stranger a drink," the freshman said with a wink. "My name's Horatio." He held his hand out to Trish. "What's yours?"

"Horatio?"

"You, too?" Horatio laughed. "Can you believe that?"

"No, no. I'm Trish, silly." She took his hand, which of course was a mistake.

Something in the warmth of his skin, something in the grip of his fingers caught her attention. Maybe it was more than her attention. It was, without a doubt, the sexiest thing she had felt in a while.

He looked at her long enough to back that up, but released her hand when she blushed.

"We have another day in paradise!" Horatio cheered.

Trish hadn't felt she was in paradise coming into Honolulu, or driving through the warehouse district. Yet, here, at this moment, in La Mariana's, it seemed to slowly materialize. The mood in the bar was one that perfectly offset being displaced on an airplane trip. The people she found herself with were comfortably accommodating to this new feeling. New friends always take the edge off.

They sat and talked of recent adventures, ordered a pitcher of strawberry-banana smoothie and laughed at each other's jokes. Horatio's leg accidentally bumped hers under the table. She accidentally bumped his back. Life was looking up.

~~~

Mike Feeney looked at his iPhone 7 prototype as if it were lying to him. It pretended not to. He put the phone back up to his ear.

"Are you kidding? Every one of them?"

"Immigration says their documents are suspect. Could be a day, maybe two, that's what I'm hearing."

"I can't wait a day or two; I need to get this sailboat delivered tomorrow." Feeney looked up at the unusual southerly drift of the clouds. "I've got a following sea right now!"

"Where are you now?" The boat broker in Los Angeles seemed to be focused on something else. Girls could be heard giggling close by.

Feeney figured the conversation was over for all practical purposes anyhow, and hung up. He walked into La Mariana and ordered a Hinano from the bar.

~~~

Horatio had his camera out, showing hiking pictures to Trish. She was amazed at the adventures these four people had been on: camping in bamboo forests, swimming in hidden pools, swinging from trees.

"This waterfall..." he began to whisper. His backpacking friends leaned in as he showed them all the image, "... convinced me of two very important things."

Trish held up a finger. "OK, number one is what?" She playfully nudged his leg with hers under the table.

Horatio moved off the bench seating and stood up next to the table, facing his friends. "One. I was a Tarzan-like ape man in a previous life!"

With that proclamation he began beating his chest and voicing the best Tarzan yell anyone there had ever heard. The people at the bar looked over and began to clap. Horatio turned and bowed to them, then looked at Trish with a slowly fading smile.

"Bravo! Bravo!" His table was clapping as well.

"And, two?" Trish asked, watching his smile slide away.

He glanced at everyone individually, catching their eye for a brief moment. "Two. That I don't want to leave."

Trish felt her heart jump at that admission. She had fought the thought since leaving Hanalei, refusing to even think it. Now, this increasingly interesting man was vocalizing it for himself, and her.

He slid back onto the bench seating, pushing closer to Trish this time. No one said a word. Everyone nodded in agreement, looking down into their glasses. Their smoothies, delicious as they had been, were almost gone.

~~~

Mike Feeney, his Hinano having worked its refreshing magic, still had a problem to solve. He needed a crew to take the 65' sailboat out of the marina here and off for delivery. His bonus required an on-time arrival.

The four drinkers at the bar were far too sauced to help. He turned to look at Tarzan and his friends across the restaurant. When he saw their backpacks, he smiled.

"They'll be up for some adventure," he said to himself, walking briskly in their direction.

~~~

Trish saw him first.

He walked with a swagger, like a Johnny Depp pirate but without the beads in his hair. Before she could alert her quiet friends to approaching company, he was standing next to their table.

"I like that, smoothies. Far healthier than ethanol," Feeney proclaimed in a hearty, booming voice.

Horatio reached out to shake his hand. "Buy us another pitcher and you can join us!"

"Captain Feeney," Mike said, looking Horatio in the eye as they battled to see who would squeeze the other man's hand the firmest. "I was hoping you would join me instead."

The five at the table looked at each other then turned to watch Feeney pull a chair over.

"My Tahitian crew couldn't clear Immigration. I've got to move a sailboat, tonight. I can pay you handsomely." He leaned back in his chair, balancing on the back two legs, arms folded in victory across his chest. He waited for their next question.

Horatio bit. "Where to, Captain?" He slid his hand under the table to find Trish's. She grabbed it and held on tightly.

"Not far, really. We'll be there just after dawn," Feeney said and grinned. Sitting his chair down, he leaned forward to study his new crew. "A little bay called Hanalei, you may have heard of it."

~~~

Trish watched her four new friends load their backpacks onto Feeney's sailboat. She stood at the dock, her small pack draped over her shoulder.

Her excuses were coming fast.

"Won't you lose your plane tickets home if you don't show at the airport?"

Horatio shrugged his shoulders. "They'll probably delay it again, anyhow. They seem to be short a few planes." He looked up at Trish standing on the dock, her hands defiantly on her hips.

"I don't know why you seem so hell bent on going back to Chicago, in January." He was losing the battle to mask his frustration at losing what he was hoping would be a special friend.

"Oh, a little something called a job. You know. J.O.B." Trish turned her back to the boat, afraid her eyes would spill the water pooling there.

One of the girls in Horatio's group saw quite clearly the sparks battling each other between him and Trish. She already had all of her stuff stowed. Walking over, she patted Horatio on the back. "This is a J.O.B. I've got friends that crew boats all over the Pacific. Not a bad gig."

She caught Trish's eye, as she turned around again. Winking, she hugged Horatio and went aft to help Feeney with fueling. It was difficult to tell if that hug was meant to discourage or prompt her, but Trish dismissed it.

"How long are you guys going to stay? I mean, you just left Kauai."

Horatio let the bow rope drop to the deck and raised his hands up in the air, as if such a question was meaningless. "Waterfall? Remember?" He began beating his chest again, channeling Tarzan with every decibel he could muster.

Trish stared at him, mystified. Was he really this charismatic or was it a touch of crazy? Maybe she was the one being crazy, discussing an adventure she knew was impossible. She switched her pack to the other shoulder and looked away, trying to focus. It took a long moment to figure out what she was supposed to be focusing on. Chicago, oh, yeah. In January.

"Five minutes, kids!" Captain Feeney announced. "We need to be sailing before sunset."

Trish turned to look nervously at Horatio. He was already staring at her, holding up five fingers. Slowly, he folded one finger down, leaving four, then another, and another until he had only one extended. That one he pointed at Trish, wiggled it a little, then pointed it back to his own heart.

"Cast the stern line!" Captain Feeney barked. One of the girls of the new crew threw it perfectly back up onto the dock. She stood now, watching Trish.

"Bow line!"

Horatio threw this one himself, letting it land close to Trish's feet. She glanced down just as she heard the sailboat's motor fire up. When she looked back up at Horatio he was pulling his shirt up and over his head, throwing it to the deck.

"Shit," Trish murmured to herself. He was beautiful. Tan, slim build and with enough muscle to hold her forever. He held out his arms to her, as the boat slowly moved away from the dock.

Everyone was watching her, wondering if the stranger they had met in the Honolulu airport was capable. Capable of changing her life in the few seconds she had left. Capable of jumping the distance between the dock and the sailboat.

"I'm in!" Trish yelled, tossing her pack into Horatio's hands and leaping.

~~~

She missed, splashing into the water just as her hands slapped the side of the boat.

"Man overboard!" Captain Feeney laughed. His stopped his engines. "Put the ladder over!"

Horatio didn't wait for such formalities. He was already in the water, swimming next to Trish, helping her toward the offered ladder. "Drama queen," he teased.

Trish grabbed a rung with one hand. She put the other around Horatio's neck and pulled him in close. "Just call me Jane."

Once everyone was properly on board and the ladder was stowed, Captain Feeney plugged his iPhone 7 prototype into the shipboard stereo system, turning up the music fashionably loud. He steered the sailboat slowly out to the pass.

"Let's dance, mateys!"

~~~

All evening, Hanalei's roosters crowed. Whatever, whomever they were summoning apparently required an extraordinary effort. The waning moon managed to keep an extra amount of glow falling onto the valley. It too felt compelled to step it up as well. The mood within the great mountain peaks above it all was one of gathering together those who could appreciate them, into broad welcoming arms.

Onolani was up early, with Birdman.

They held hands as both of them walked the short distance to the taro field terrace where he always played for the mountains. She knew it was a special invitation to accompany him. He was famous for being alone, but today, she would dance one of the hula he had taught her long ago.

Her dreams last night, about the tsunami and the great pulse, about her growing connection with the mystical, were transformative. She felt a wise confidence growing in her heart. The universe was opening up new venues where she could express her emotions, her worship.

As she held Birdman's warm hand in the cool predawn air, she looked up at the high cirrus clouds, already catching light and smiled. They were talking to her, telling her of amazing places she was discovering within herself. They were speaking of the wonder within this new love with her old partner, but most importantly, of the majesty all around her home here in the middle of the third planet's most wonderful of oceans.

Little Poi followed them at a distance, hopping from one terrace to another until he saw them stop. It wasn't long before he saw them hug deeply, move gently apart and begin: Birdman playing his acoustic slack-key as Onolani described with her hands how the rains of Wai'ale'ale were a gift from Heaven.

Poi couldn't agree more as he slipped into the shallow water and circled the agreeable taro plants.

~~~

The light, southerly winds that had followed Captain Feeney and crew west-northwest were turning back to tradewinds. As the sun rose they got eight knots from the northeast.

The timing was perfect, something Captain Feeney wasn't unfamiliar with but still appreciated, anyhow. It would allow him to round the island and head for Hanalei with a new following sea.

Horatio was coming up from below with more coffee. It had been a long night, but one full of entertainment to keep them awake. Flying fish, dolphins, incredibly bright stars early on and later the moon. Trish still required coffee, even as Horatio and his three friends sang to the sun.

"How are you doing?" Horatio asked, taking a break and sitting next to Trish. "Have I told you how much I love that you got on board with us - even if it took two tries?" His light laughter was infectious, even at her mild expense.

Trish sipped her coffee slowly, watching his hypnotic eyebrows rise. He had put his shirt back on long ago to weather the evening, but as the sun rose he seemed ready to peel it off again. Or, she would do it for him. After the coffee.

"I just can't believe I'm coming back," Trish let her amazement show. "Especially this way, by sea."

She was looking over his shoulders now at the towering green peaks of Kauai pushing through the tops of morning cloud cover. They appeared to be some four or five miles offshore.

"You never told me what you were *not* going back to," Trish said, sipping more of the steaming coffee.

Horatio smiled. "Three wives, eighteen kids, a commune in Montana. You know, that kind of stuff."

Trish punched him playfully in the shoulder. "Me, too."

Horatio reached over to hold a lock of her hair back from her face. "I didn't take you for the three wives type."

"No, just the commune part. A commune of one."

Horatio nodded. "You're far too beautiful not to share with someone." He leaned over to kiss her, but was met by her hand at his lips.

"Will you please take off that damn shirt first?"

~~~

Poi was trying to stomp his short little feet.

Onolani and Birdman had done it, clearing most of the mud off of them. However, he couldn't quite get enough stomp in his step to shake much off.

Birdman walked across the street to his job at the grocery. Onolani whistled for Poi and they slowly made their way to the bay, cutting through the Ching Young shopping complex, rounding the still closed whale-watching kiosks, and finally making their way to Weke street.

The warm ocean could finish cleaning both of them off.

~~~

Captain Feeney noted how his crew had begun shedding their clothes at first light. A fine crew indeed. Swimsuits had replaced airplane clothes, inviting the tropical warmth in.

He was proud of them and thrilled no one had fallen overboard in the channel between the two islands. They had performed well - in perfect weather on a moon-filled night with a following sea. Coupled with an experienced crew they might be fun on a Tahiti run.

Never one to command without example, he shed his shirt, too. That made six of them. It felt good, this warm wind and sunshine brushing against his skin. That and the spectacular view of Hanalei valley coming up made this trip worthwhile. And that bonus.

"Captain's meeting!" Feeney shouted out over the laughing and the light waves.

Trish followed the rest of them back to the helm.

"OK, listen up. First of all, great job!" Captain Feeney gave them a big thumbs up, which, as his pinkie fell away, became a shaka sign. "I'll cut checks for everyone tonight, but you have to meet me at this place called Tahiti Nui, you may have heard of it."

They, of course, all had.

"Second, I'm going to anchor close to shore, surf permitting. The new owner is going to arrive by zodiac and take over then. You can throw your gear in and they'll ferry you to shore. Good?"

Everyone nodded.

"Lastly, as Captain, I am allowed under maritime law to declare the obvious at any time I see fit."

"Hear! Hear!" Horatio followed.

"Yes," Captain Feeney continued. "I do declare that you're the finest topless crew I've ever had the pleasure to sail with on a leg from O'ahu to Kauai on a waning moon terminating in Hanalei bay! Rum smoothies on me tonight!"

"Hear! Hear!" Trish shouted, feeling a lot freer than she had in far, far too long.

"Yes, well then," Captain Feeney said, going back to holding the helm with both hands again. "Prepare the anchor in five!"

~~~

Poi had to avert his eyes from the brightly colored hibiscus all along the road. The yellows, the reds and the double pinks were too much for him. Greens and blues he could handle, but the bright rainbow hues were too much to process. Onolani's pareo was difficult to follow without having to look away often. This morning, he followed her pikake perfume scent whenever she got too far ahead of him.

"Come on, big boy!" Onolani turned back, waving at him.

He loved it so much when she pronounced his name correctly on her first try. The conflict was whether to stay and wag his butt furiously in happiness, or run ahead toward her. He couldn't do both at the same time. He decided to take turns. He wagged real quick, relishing the happiness flowing through him as he did, then just as quickly stopped. As soon as his butt settled, he put his head down a little and ran full speed ahead.

"That's my boy!" Onolani said, bending down to catch him.

Ah! She had said his name correctly, again! While he was in mid-stride! His butt was trying to wiggle now, throwing off his balance, while he was in a high speed power run! It was only with the focus of an Olympian that he managed to keep from tumbling completely out of control.

Onolani picked him up, letting him kiss her with his exuberant tongue. First, he got her cheeks, then her closed eyes as she laughed, and finally, up her nostril. It was a mystery to him while she didn't like that one the best. It was certainly his favorite.

Still cradling him, on his back, Onolani turned the corner into the beach park. She rubbed his little-dog belly. His right leg always lost all control when she did that, moving in a horse trot all by itself. He was sure it made him look ridiculous.

"Hey, look there, Poi. A sailboat!"

~ ~ ~

Trish stood at the bow as they slowly entered Hanalei bay. The mountains in the background, the two or three waterfalls peeling down between the ridges, and the long crescent beach all seemed to be happy to see her.

The surf was unusually small for this time of year, allowing Captain Feeney to get within fifty yards of the shoreline.

"Anchors aweigh!" he commanded. The boat was coasting along at about four knots.

Horatio cast the seventy-five pound sand anchor over the side, stepping out of the last loop right before it swooped over and into the clear, colorless shallows.

Trish stood poised, her toes already over the edge, ready to dive gracefully into the bay. She was hopeful that Horatio would soon join her and they could dive in together. It would be just perfect, both of them entering paradise from a tropical sea...

The anchor caught hold of a large lava rock and quickly started tightening the slack line. Captain Feeney felt the first slipping tug on the boat, and reached for the railing. No one else did. An instant later the sailboat stopped moving altogether, jerking to a stop.

When Horatio looked up he saw Trish flailing backwards in mid air, already swimming with her arms.

~~~

Poi was anxious to do his customary long beach walk. Onolani didn't have the energy. Between Birdman at night, Birdman in the morning, and no opportunity to take a nap lately, she was exhausted. She propped herself against a short coconut palm and watched the bay again, letting her tired eyes gently lead her into daydreams.

A familiar looking neighbor was jogging by with her English bulldog. He had been nice enough to Poi on the street before, and his owner was actually running! Perfect! Poi ran off after them, pacing them off to the side as they continued out of sight.

Onolani looked up for a moment, saw Poi off with friends and then noticed the sailboat again. A zodiac approached it, offloaded and then loaded something. Wouldn't it be nice, she thought, if someone would bring her a gift from some faraway place? Something unique and wonderful.

Kauai's charm was its isolation, but it was also its limitation. If it wasn't for the tourists, she was sure, Hanalei wouldn't have any conveniences at all. As it was, they rarely saw anything that wasn't made in China or distributed through Costco. Their own unique artists did a great job, but no art from Lebanon or Paris or even Lake Tahoe ever made it to Hanalei.

Maybe that was what forced her sister to leave. Chicago had everything, times ten. That was a mighty powerful incentive to return, she figured. Yet, Trish had indicated, mostly through her embracing of Poi, a spiritual side as well. That had probably been what had angered Onolani the most. Her sister had the magic, too. All she needed was some guidance, some training and she too could do great things, teach the wonders of beauty to others.

Onolani opened her eyes and scanned the waters in front of her. She knew Trish should be back at her apartment in Chicago by now, yet, that didn't feel right. Subtle hints were telling her something had changed.

She closed her eyes. Breathing in deeply and slowly, Onolani opened her mind and reached out into the vast waters again. Just as she had searched for the great earthquake pulse, so she now felt for a likeness to her own.

~~~

Embarrassed, again, Trish waved off any help.

"I'm going to swim in," she told Horatio. "See you at Tahiti Nui?"

"I'll save you a seat," he yelled back. As much as he wanted to follow her in, he still had the backpacker code to follow. He couldn't abandon his original crew. They might adopt a member, but they could never split apart. Not until they all made it home.

Horatio looked at a new part of his heart swimming in toward shore and wondered if this crescent beach, this wonderful slice of amazing, would be a new home for him. And, perhaps, for Trish.

He turned to help load up the zodiac.

The warm water sliding over Trish was almost electric. It moved across her skin, but something in it went deeper. Like a mother's caress of her new baby, a touch of love confirming "you are of me". She shuddered a little under the weight of compassion flooding into her mind, welcoming her back. Home.

Her eyes warmed with tears as the sea kissed them away. They mixed with the countless others before her, stirring gently as she swam slowly to shore. The touch of the waters was holding her up, lifting her toward the sky, preparing her to listen.

It spoke softly to her, trying to explain. This magical place here, that you rejected, is giving you an opportunity to try again - to try and find that special spiritual quality of peace, some sliver of personal happiness that has so far eluded your hippie soul.

Trish stopped swimming, her tears turning to sobs, making it impossible to continue. Treading water easily, she let her emotions finish. She looked to the blue in the sky above, shimmering under her tears. The sun there felt warm under her hot tears, promising to show her how majestic she really was.

"Yes!" Trish yelled to the sky. "I want to see it all!"

She soon moved again toward the shore, kicking her legs, laying on her back, and watching the tiny giggling clouds race ahead to play in the crown of the Island. If only, Trish thought, she could explain this feeling to her sister. She would know what it meant.

When she felt the water become shallow, she flipped herself over, planting her feet in the submerged sand. Trish stood and looked ahead. There, barefoot in the beautiful wash of waves, holding her arms out to her, stood a most radiant Onolani.

~~~

Trish froze for a moment. This vision appeared to be her sister, but... how could it be? She was angelic, almost floating in an aura of soft, glowing sunshine. Trish rubbed her eyes free of tears and ocean, hearing as she did, "we have so much to talk about".

Clear-eyed, she walked toward her sister, still several yards away. Trish was beaming. She wasn't sure if she said yes, or just thought it, but Onolani nodded.

"Welcome home," Onolani soon whispered into her ear, hugging her sister. "I don't know how to tell you just how amazing this is."

"It's a bit of a story, Ono."

Onolani kissed her hair and held her out at arm's length. "I can imagine, starting with your new swimming attire, or lack of." Onolani laughed out loud.

Unabashed now, Trish felt good. "Law of the sea, or so I've been told."

In the distance, hidden just below the sheeting swish of water on the sand and the wind rustling coconut fronds there was a frantic barking in the near distance. Fast approaching from down the beach, Trish turned to see what it might be.

Using the innate advantage of short legs, powerful muscles built specifically for maximum speed, Poi rocketed ahead of his escort. He knew he had never been this fast before. Chickens pecking for bugs in the shades of the trees took notice of the respectable rooster-tail the little dog was generating behind him.

"Poi boy!" Trish yelled, jumping up and down as the low, dark mass approached at an unstoppable speed.

"Watch out..." Onolani laughed, just as Poi overshot them, tried to turn, but tumbled once, twice, three times. Quickly getting up, uninterested in shaking off the coating of sand he now had, he ran back to the sisters.

"Oh, Poi. I am so glad to see you." Trish tried to reach down and pet him. It was impossible. He kept wiggling his little butt so furiously that it was knocking him off balance. Getting back up after each fall, he continued wagging and would fall yet again.

Trish finally rescued him from his enthusiasm and picked the little dog up, letting him lick her face. Hugging him tightly, she looked all around, at the mountains, the ocean, her sister.

"I love you, too!"

more novels at

everett.peacock.com